Those who have crossed
With direct eyes, to death's other Kingdom
Remember us – if at all – not as lost
Violent souls, but only
As the hollow men

TS Eliot, *The Hollow Men*

CONTENTS
PART ONE: TARNAGAR

PART TWO: MOITEERA

Part One
TARNAGAR

In dreams begins responsibility

WB Yeats

AN ACCIDENT IN THE KITCHEN

When Dante Cazabon used his shoulder to open the double doors of the kitchen, he was concentrating on the mountain of soup bowls he carried on a tray in front of him. He was thinking that the bowls had been scraped so clean by the inmates of Corridor Y, they scarcely needed washing. This was because the inmates of Corridor Y, like every other inmate in the asylum, received only as much food as was considered good for them. Whenever Dante arrived with their meals, therefore, they regarded him with a hungry and accusing look that made it very clear they wanted more. Unfortunately, Dante could only follow orders.

Following orders was Dante's life. Some people gave orders; others followed them. That was the way things were done in the asylum. There was a very strict chain of command. At the top was the director. The ordinary workers only caught an occasional glimpse of his pale, thin form, gliding about the corridors, surrounded by secretaries and bodyguards. Beneath him were the medical staff in their white coats. Then came the administrators, carrying their clipboards and checking their watches to make sure that everything was as it should be. Next in line were the functionaries who oiled the wheels of the machine and made sure its great creaking structure continued to work on a daily basis: the cooks and cleaners, carpenters and plumbers, gardeners, groundsmen and jacks of all trades. Below them were the security staff, burly men and women in their blue uniforms, who guaranteed the safety of the outside world by ensuring that neither staff nor inmates ever went beyond the walls of the asylum without permission. And at the very bottom of the pile was Dante.

He was the lowest of the low – the child of an inmate. And not just any inmate. His mother had been one of the asylum's most dangerous and unpredictable patients. She had thrown herself from the top of the Great Tower when Dante was just a baby. Her smashed body had been found on the cobblestones below in the early hours of the morning. As a result, Dante had been brought up by asylum staff, and from his earliest days he had been taught to be grateful for the privilege.

His childhood had not been an easy one. No one had ever picked him up and cuddled him, telling him that he was their own little darling. Treatment like this was reserved for other children. Dante had learned to be thankful for any crumb of affection that was thrown his way but, on the whole, not very many were. He had been granted his own tiny room above the kitchen, and just enough food to live on. In return, he was expected to do the jobs that other people didn't like to think about.

If a violently disturbed inmate improvised some kind

of weapon and managed to spill her own blood, it was Dante who cleared up the mess. If someone was found hanging from the ceiling by the cord of his pyjamas, eyes bulging and tongue sticking out, it was Dante who cut him down. If there were slops to be emptied, stains to be removed, unpleasant sights to be swept away, Dante was given the task. And he was not expected to whine about it.

So when a foot snaked out just as he was stepping through the kitchen doors, tripping him up and sending forty-seven soup bowls flying through the air to land on the hard stone slabs and shatter into a thousand pieces, Dante did not complain. He went sprawling forward, hitting his knee against the great wooden bench that ran down the middle of the room with a force that sent waves of pain running up and down his leg, but he still remained silent.

A gale of laughter from the other kitchen workers was followed almost immediately by a string of curses from Mr Cuddy, the portly catering manager.

'You clumsy fool!' he shouted, hitting Dante as hard as he could with the flat of his hand.

Dante's head rocked backwards and stars burst into life before his eyes.

'Clear it up!' Mr Cuddy barked.

'Yes, sir,' Dante muttered. Out of the corner of his eye he saw the lanky form of Jerome Mazarin, the cook's first assistant, lounging against the wall beside the doorframe, his hatchet-face contorted into a grin of delight. Jerome took considerable delight in making life difficult for others, particularly Dante. On a ledge outside one of the kitchen windows he kept a glass jar with a little honey smeared inside it, to trap insects so that during his leisure time he could pull off their wings or their legs. Dante sighed. Ignoring the pain in his knee, he began to collect the broken soup bowls and put them in the bin.

If he had paused, looked up from the broken shards of crockery and peered out of the window, he would have seen a tall girl, with dark wavy hair cascading down the back of her long white dress. She was walking determinedly across the lawn of the asylum's West Wing under the shadow of the Great Tower, clutching a leather-bound book in one hand and frowning sternly.

Beatrice Argenti was thinking, as she often did, that the asylum was a particularly ugly and dispiriting place in which to live. The Old Clinic at its centre, with its gargoyles and turrets, had a certain style, though it could never have been described as beautiful, but it was surrounded by the most ramshackle collection of buildings imaginable. Rows and rows of mean little houses in which the medical staff and administrators lived, then the larger communal halls of residence for the more lowly workers. These gave way to a great jumble of offices and workshops, garages and outbuildings that straggled down to the woods. Beyond the woods, the Outer Wall encircled the grounds. The whole thing was like some dreadful, nameless beast, squatting in the centre of the island, its poisonous tentacles stretching out to encompass every blade of grass and every last inch of rock.

If Bea had been able to choose a life for herself it would have been quite different. She would not have been born in an asylum on the remote island of Tarnagar. She would not have picked two very dull and dutiful junior doctors for her parents. And there would have been no coming-of-age ceremony.

She made a face as she contemplated this. The thought of the ceremony troubled her mind like a splinter troubles the body. If she could talk about how she felt perhaps it would be easier to bear. But who was there to discuss it with? Her mother would just smile patiently and tell her that every young person feels nervous when the great day approaches. 'It's perfectly natural,' she would insist in that infuriatingly calm voice of hers. 'Once the ceremony is over you'll feel quite different.' Her father would probably treat her to a long and tedious lecture about the importance of developing 'a positive attitude'.

She had crossed the lawn by now and was making her way among big, old trees, following the little stream that ran through the asylum's grounds and out under the wall. Bea envied that stream. It could go where it chose ,unhindered by rules and regulations.

She sought out her favourite tree, an ancient willow so bent over that its branches grew parallel to the ground and were low enough to sit on. There she opened the leather-bound book and began to read aloud the words she was supposed to have learnt by heart: 'Dr Sigmundus has promised us that where there was uncertainty, there shall be reassurance, where there was anxiety, there shall be peace.'

She closed the book again. How tired she was of hearing what Dr Sigmundus had to say! Involuntarily, she glanced about her as she thought this. It was dangerous even to think such things. Sometimes she felt sure that other people could read her mind and see the treacherous sentiments she nourished there.

Why was she so different from all the other young people she knew? Francesca Belmonti, who had been born on the same day – barely two hours earlier in fact – was looking forward to her coming-of-age ceremony with a ferocious intensity. She talked about nothing else but the dress her mother had ordered from the mainland, the party that was being planned to celebrate the occasion, the food that would be eaten at the party, which guests would be invited and which would not. Bea, on the other hand, had told her mother she did not want a party. She might as well have saved her breath. Her mother had simply nodded as if she agreed perfectly with what her daughter had said. 'We will just have a little party,' she told Bea. 'Only our closest friends will be invited.'

The very idea was ridiculous! There was no such thing as a little party on Tarnagar. Whether Bea liked it or not, all her parents' colleagues would come with their dreadful sons and daughters in tow. The adults would stand around talking about work. Their children would try to outdo each other with stories of how much had already been spent, and how much was still going to be spent, on their coming-of-age ceremonies. It sometimes seemed to Bea that all anyone on Tarnagar ever thought about was whether they were more or less important than the person they were talking to.

Of course Bea knew perfectly well that there was no point in thinking like this. However much she hated the idea, she could not avoid turning fourteen in four weeks time and she would have to learn the words of the ceremony. Otherwise there would be another family row, and she could predict exactly how it would develop. Her mother would put on her reasonable voice, her father would put on his stern voice and Bea would put on her defiant voice. Then they would all argue for hours on end until her father finally lost his temper and ended up ordering Bea to her room. She sighed, opened the book again and began to recite the Promises of Dr Sigmundus.

A CHANCE MEETING

Once he had disposed of the remains of the broken soup bowls, Dante began to tackle the huge pile of washing-up. Now that the joke was over and there was no more pleasure to be gained from watching him writhing in pain, the others quickly lost interest and returned to their work.

Mr Cuddy went to talk to Mrs Boxer, the laundry mistress, about a batch of uniforms that had just come back from the wash. In his opinion they were far from satisfactory. Marsyas, the cook, began pounding steaks on a chopping board. He was a big, ugly man whose face seemed to have been assembled from a whole series of different individuals. His left ear, for example, was significantly larger than his right, and whenever he was angry it turned bright red and seemed to swell to an even greater size. Today, however, he was in a surprisingly good humour and he hummed to himself as he worked. Meanwhile his three assistants busied themselves chopping vegetables.

'New patient's coming tomorrow,' said Nathaniel, the second assistant, a short, stocky young man. Though no more than twenty-five, he was completely bald and the top of his head shone where he rubbed pig's grease into it every morning, in the vain hope that it would make the hair re-grow. The recipe for this cure had apparently been suggested to him by Polly, Mrs Boxer's assistant, who had found it in an old book of tips for housekeepers. No one else believed in it but Nathaniel was known to be sweet on Polly. Besides, there was always plenty of pig's grease going spare in the kitchen.

'What's his name?' asked Ivan, the third assistant. He had dark hair and a ready smile. He might have been handsome had not the left side of his face been badly scarred from an accident with a pan of boiling water when he was a boy.

'Ezekiel something,' Nathaniel said.

'Ezekiel Semiramis,' Jerome told them.

'They say he's the most dangerous patient we've ever had,' Nathaniel went on.

'What's he done then?' Ivan asked.

'What hasn't he done?' Nathaniel replied. 'Killed hundreds, they reckon.'

'Tortured people, that's what I've heard,' Jerome said, smiling to himself as if the idea gave him pleasure.

Dante took no part in this, or in any other kitchen conversation. Anything he had to say would almost certainly have been scorned. He worked his way steadily through the washing-up and kept his eye out for an opportunity to slip away. One of the very few advantages of his position was that he had no fixed responsibilities. No one else who worked in the asylum could say the same. Indeed, they cherished their responsibilities.

Mr Cuddy was responsible for the running of the kitchen, the purchasing of supplies, the provision of knives and forks, plates and spoons, bowls, dishes, mugs and every other item of kitchenware. Mrs Boxer was responsible for the cleanliness of towels and uniforms, sheets and blankets, tablecloths, bedspreads and curtains. Marsyas was responsible for the quality, flavour and wholesomeness of meals. His assistants were responsible for the preparation of ingredients. Dante, on the other hand, was responsible for nothing. He was simply expected to perform whatever tasks were given to him.

Whether Mr Cuddy wanted him to polish the napkin rings for the director's table, Mrs Boxer needed him to bring in a line of washing from the rain, or Marsyas required him to take a bucket of scraps to the kennels, Dante was expected to oblige. The positive side of it, however, was that no one was entirely sure where he ought to be at any given time.

When he had finished the washing-up, he picked up a bucket and mop and went out through the door that led to the back corridor. As soon as he was out of sight, he put the mop and bucket down in a corner where no one was likely to see them, and slipped out through the little door that led into the yard where the rubbish bins were kept.

The rubbish bins were overflowing with kitchen waste, and even Dante, who was used to noxious smells, had to hold his nose as he walked past. Out of the corner of his eye he noticed an enormous rat, sitting on top of one of the bins, feasting on a heap of vegetable peelings, rotten fruit and fish skin.

Once out of the yard, he headed for the woods. The quickest way was to follow the path around the Old Clinic and then make his way across the lawn. But if he chose that route, he would probably be spotted. Besides, it would mean crossing the cobbles beneath the Great Tower where his mother had met her end, and this was something Dante preferred to avoid. So he made his way through the kitchen gardens instead, past the lines of fruit bushes. It was longer, but safer and less fraught with treacherous associations.

In a few months these bushes would be laden with berries. More than once in the past Dante had helped himself to a handful and he could clearly remember the taste – sharp and earthy at the same time. But he never got very many. The best of the crop was always picked and served with cream at the director's table. What was left over was eaten by the senior staff.

Beyond the kitchen gardens was a strip of scrubland and then the woods began. Once he was among the trees, Dante felt safe enough to stop, pull up the leg of his trousers and examine his knee. The skin was already turning blue. He pressed the tender part gently with his finger and the pain almost made him cry out loud. The memory of Jerome's long, thin face with its grin of satisfaction came into his mind and anger flared up inside him. But it did not last. Dante could never feel angry for very long. Jerome was pathetic, really. None of the other kitchen staff liked him, even if they did laugh at his jokes.

What Dante mostly felt on occasions like this was a great sense of loneliness. He found himself thinking about his mother and wondering why someone would contrive such a dreadful end for themselves. She must have been driven to it by unbearable mental anguish. The thought of that suffering only added to the sadness weighing him down.

He forced himself to push these thoughts to the back of his mind and concentrated on looking for a piece of wood suitable for carving. Mostly, he had to make do with fallen branches that were half-rotten and fell to pieces under the knife, but every now and again he came across something with real potential. Occasionally the trees were thinned by the groundstaff to keep the woods manageable, and the men who did the job often left cross-sections of the thicker branches lying about. Some of these were just the right size. Alternatively, one of the smaller trees might get blown down in a gale and, if he was lucky, he would find a broken bough that was still sound.

On the window ledge in his room, he had assembled a little collection of carvings. They ranged from his very first – a crude wooden spoon – to his most recent, a man's head with one ear bigger than the other. There was no doubt about it, he had a talent for carving and he was becoming better at it the more he practised, though all he had to work with were a couple of knives he had filched from the kitchen. No one else had ever seen his handiwork. The other kitchen workers didn't think he could do anything except carry trays of food up and down stairs and peel potatoes but if they'd seen his likeness of Marsyas they might have changed their minds.

It was while he was thinking about this that he noticed the girl. She was sitting by herself on the branch of a tree reading aloud from a book. He stood perfectly still, held his breath and listened.

'Let us give thanks for the gift of contentment,' she intoned. 'Let us be grateful for the release from yearning. Let us acknowledge the great benefactor of mankind. Let us give praise to Dr Sigmundus.'

Dante knew these words very well. He had spoken them himself nearly a year ago. Since he could not read, never having been to school, he had been unable to learn them from a book. Instead, he had been allowed to repeat them after Mr Cuddy, who had been the sponsor at his coming-of-age ceremony. But he remembered speaking them – and thinking, at the same time, that they were all lies.

Unaware that she was being watched, the girl covered the page with her hand and began again, this time trying to recall the words unprompted. Halfway through, she realised that she had got the sentences in the wrong order and stopped.

'Oh, who cares about bloody Dr Sigmundus, anyway!' she said.

She had such a polite, well-brought-up accent, and was clearly so unused to even the mildest swearing that Dante couldn't help laughing out loud. Immediately, the

23

girl looked up and saw him.

'What do you think you're doing spying on me?' she demanded, angrily.

Dante was taken aback. 'I wasn't spying,' he replied.

'Yes, you were.'

'I was just walking along when I saw you.'

Bea was not at all sure that she believed him. This was her spot. No one else ever came here. What was he doing here, anyway? She looked at him more closely. He was thin and pale with fair hair and very blue eyes. She remembered seeing him going about the asylum from time to time and suspected that he was one of the kitchen staff. Had he overheard what she had been saying?

'If you think anyone's going to listen to what you say about me, then you're wrong,' she told him. 'You're only a kitchen boy. My parents are doctors.'

Even as she spoke, she knew that she sounded exactly like the sort of person she scorned, someone who spent all their time trying to make others believe they were inferior. But the words were out of her mouth before she had a chance to think about them.

Dante nodded. 'You're quite right,' he said softly. Then he turned and began to walk away.

'Wait!' Bea called out.

Dante stopped and turned to look at her.

'I'm sorry,' she said. 'I shouldn't have said that.'

Dante shrugged. 'It doesn't matter,' he said. 'It's true, anyway. Nobody's going to listen to me.'

'Even if it is true, it was still a horrible thing to say,'

24

Bea admitted. 'It's just that you startled me. I didn't expect to meet anyone. No one else ever comes here except me.'

'I do,' Dante said.

'I've never seen you here before.'

'Well, I've never seen you here before.'

Bea hesitated. She had the feeling that if she wanted to patch things up, then it was up to her to continue. 'Your name's Dante, isn't it?' she asked.

'Yes.'

'I'm Bea.'

Dante nodded, though he still did not seem mollified.

But Bea was determined now and once her mind was made up, she was not easily put off. She thought for a moment, then remembered something that might interest him. 'There's a badger's sett, near here,' she said. 'Have you seen it?'

'I didn't know there were any badgers in these woods,' Dante replied.

'There are lots of them. I've seen them. I climbed out of my bedroom window and came here in the early hours of the morning. I kept downwind and crept up very quietly. There was a whole family, rolling about and playing together. Then they heard me and vanished.'

Dante smiled faintly. She sounded so proud of herself. He suspected that she was the sort of person who enjoyed doing things in secret.

'I'll show you where it is if you like.'

Still uncertain, he nodded and she led the way

through the trees. Walking slightly behind her, he had the chance to study her more carefully. She could not have been described as pretty but she was certainly striking, with dark eyes that seemed full of hidden depths. The bottom of her dress was caked with mud and he wondered whether she would get into trouble when she got home. Probably not. He suspected that she was too clever for that.

They came out in a clearing, where she suddenly stopped and cried out in dismay. As Dante drew level with her, he saw the body of a young badger on the ground. It had been caught in a trap and had clearly been dead for some time. There was dried blood on it and flies were buzzing around its eyes. Bea stared at it in horror, tears running down her face.

Dante put his hand on her arm. 'Come on,' he said. 'There's nothing we can do here.'

Reluctantly, Bea allowed herself to be led away. 'Why did they have to do that?' she demanded.

'Because that's what people are like,' Dante said.

'I thought Ichor was supposed to have stopped all that,' Bea pointed out. 'Violence and aggression, I mean.'

'Ichor just makes people easier to control,' Dante said. 'They don't question their orders. So they don't have the urge to, say, start a war. But they still enjoy being cruel.' He sat down on a fallen log and Bea perched on a tree stump opposite. 'When's your coming-of-age ceremony?' he asked.

She made a face. 'Four weeks from today.'

'Aren't you looking forward to it?'

She gave him a withering look. 'That's all anyone ever says: aren't you looking forward to it? Well I'm not looking forward to it, not one bit.'

'I thought you'd be having a big party, and everything,' Dante went on. 'Isn't that what people do?'

'I don't want a big party and everything,' Bea told him. 'And I don't want to receive Ichor, either.' It was not the sort of thing well-brought-up girls ought to say and Bea studied Dante's face to see how he would react. She waited for him to tell her that it was perfectly natural to feel anxious before your coming-of-age ceremony but that once you received Ichor everything would be just fine. But he didn't say that. Instead, he said the very last thing she would have expected anyone to say.

'I didn't want to take it, either,' he told her. 'It didn't matter in the end anyway, because Ichor doesn't work on me.'

She looked at him incredulously. 'How do you know?'

Even though they were on their own in the middle of the woods, Dante looked around, making sure there was no one who might overhear him. Then he leaned forward and, lowering his voice, said, 'I still have dreams.'

Bea gasped. This was the most shocking thing anyone had ever said to her. One part of her wanted to turn and run away. But another part, the part that cherished secrets, would not let her move. Finally she spoke.

'Dr Sigmundus says that disturbances of the mind which come to people when they sleep are the result of psychic illness.' It was what she had been taught at school, and for as long as she could remember.

Dante shrugged. 'Who cares about bloody Dr Sigmundus, anyway!' he said. He grinned and, despite herself, Bea grinned back. Suddenly, the silence that hung over the woods was broken by the sound of the bell in the Great Tower, tolling the hour. Bea started, remembering her appointment with the dressmaker.

'I've got to go,' she said.

She could not say for sure but she thought that Dante looked...disappointed. At least she hoped he did.

She held out her hand. 'It was nice to meet you,' she told him.

Dante looked at her hand for a moment as if he was not sure what to do with it. Then he reached out and clasped it. 'You too, Bea,' he replied.

After she had gone Dante stood for a little while looking after her. She was an odd girl, but he liked her. There was an honesty about her that he had never encountered in anyone. As he was thinking this, he noticed a sheet of paper lying on the ground next to the tree stump on which she'd been sitting. It must have dropped out of her book. It was a drawing, done with pencil. He turned it the right side up and saw that it was a picture of a girl standing beside a tall stone tower. The girl was Bea, but Dante did not recognise her surroundings. All around her were fallen masonry, gaping windows and collapsed walls. It was as though she were in the midst of a ruined city.

He stood there for some time, studying the picture

until it occurred to him that he had been missing for too long. Somebody was bound to be looking for him by now. He didn't want to damage the drawing by folding it, so he hid it inside his shirt, then set off back to the kitchen, ready to follow orders once again.

THE NEW PATIENT

It was Nathaniel who brought the news. He came back from the cheese store with a full round cheddar in his hands and a look of nervous fascination on his face.

'The new patient's arrived,' he announced. 'Ezekiel whatshisname.'

As if by unspoken agreement, everyone in the kitchen stopped work, filed out the back door and made their way to the front entrance.

There was already quite a crowd: a few of the more junior clerks, a small group of nurses and orderlies, a cluster of maintenance staff and cleaners, all standing in their separate groups. The inhabitants of Tarnagar did not mix beyond their appointed ranks. The consultants and senior administrators weren't there, of course. They considered it beneath their dignity to be seen in such a gathering. Nevertheless, one or two eminent faces could be glimpsed peering from the second-floor window. Conversation died down completely as a guard unlocked the back doors of the big black van used to transport patients and Ezekiel Semiramis stepped out into the daylight.

He was smaller than Dante had expected, and slighter, too. It was hard to tell how old he was – forty-five perhaps? There was grey in his hair and his face was lined, but there was something youthful about him as well. Now that Dante looked more closely, he could see the man's face was bruised. Had he put up a fight when they captured him? His arms were handcuffed in front of him but he held his head up proudly, looking with an air of defiance at the gawking crowd. When his gaze fell on Dante, however, his expression seemed to change, as if he had found what he had been looking for. One of the security guards gave him a prod with the end of his baton and the little procession of patient and warders made its way across the gravel drive and through the main doors of the clinic.

Afterwards, as the workers all trooped reluctantly back to their various stations, Dante wondered about that look. Had he imagined it? After all, no one else had mentioned it. Instead, Nathaniel and Ivan talked cheerfully about what an evil face the new patient had.

'Anyone can tell he's a killer,' Nathaniel said.

'Smaller than I expected, though,' Ivan pointed out.

'Those are the ones you have to watch,' Nathaniel assured him. 'They've got a grudge against the world, see. They hate the rest of us for being normal.'

'There's nothing normal about you two,' Jerome cut in. 'He's got a face like a side of bacon and you've got a head like a billiard cue.'

Neither of them replied. They knew better than to try to take on Jerome in a battle of wits.

The bell in the Old Tower was tolling eleven o'clock when they got back to the kitchen. The patients had all

31

been brought their meals three hours ago; the empty plates had been collected, washed, dried and put away. Dante's job for the rest of the morning was washing potatoes. The head gardener had delivered a barrel-load to the kitchen door the previous day. But the last few weeks had been very wet and the potatoes were caked with mud.

The worst thing about this chore was the cold water. The asylum's hot water supply was notoriously unreliable so hot water was rationed. Dante's hands soon began to ache and he had to keep stopping to warm them under his armpits. But at least he was outside and by himself, unless you counted the rats. One of the farm workers had come and taken away the kitchen waste for the pigs earlier that morning. But the rats still hung about, sniffing the air hopefully.

Dante ignored them. He plunged his hands yet again into the barrel of muddy potatoes and thought about Ezekiel Semiramis. The majority of the patients in the asylum were entirely harmless, sitting and staring at the walls all day. The doctors put them through a set of tests every month and methodically recorded their progress on charts but nothing about their behaviour ever changed. They would die as they had lived, hardly aware of what was happening to them.

But there was a minority of unpredictable patients. Most of the time they remained docile, but every now and again they would become possessed by an unreasoning fury. Then they would hammer on the doors of their cells and scream to be let out. Sometimes they would injure themselves, banging their heads against the walls until they knocked themselves unconscious. Of these unpredictable cases, a handful were a danger to others as well as themselves. No chances were taken with them. Though they were restrained by manacles, Dante still felt uneasy when he brought them their meals.

If the rumours were correct, Ezekiel Semiramis belonged in this category. Patients like him received a variety of treatments. They were given special food – nothing highly flavoured. It was believed that flavourings and sweeteners could make their condition worse. Whenever they posed problems they were subjected to 'the regime'. This meant they were stripped naked, doused with freezing cold water and woken at regular intervals during the night. If this did not change their behaviour, they were taken to the Shock Room.

The Shock Room was in the heart of the Old Clinic. On the front of the door was the symbol of a lightning bolt etched in red. Once inside the room, the patient was strapped to a table, a leather gag forced between his teeth to stop him from biting his tongue, and electrodes attached to his head. Then, at the flick of a switch, hundreds of volts of electricity were passed through his brain. It was a fate Dante would have wished on no one, however violent.

It took him half the morning to work his way through the barrel of potatoes. By the end, his hands were raw, and his teeth were chattering. He was actually glad to re-enter the muggy heat of the kitchen. But as soon as he did so, the buzz of conversation died down. As he glanced around, most of his fellow workers looked away, embarrassed, but there was an expression of malicious pleasure on Jerome's face.

'Cuddy's been looking for you,' he announced.

'What have I done wrong?' Dante asked.

'Nothing, as far as I know,' Jerome replied with feigned innocence.

Just then Mr Cuddy himself came into the kitchen. 'Ah, there you are, Dante,' he said. 'I want you to take the new patient something to eat.'

So that was the big joke. They were hoping Dante would be terrified. He took a tray from the cupboard beside the door and went over to collect the plate of food Marsyas had prepared.

'You'd better watch you don't get too close to that one,' Jerome said. 'I heard he blinded a guard on the mainland. Two fingers in the man's eyes, that was all it took.' Jerome held up the first two fingers of his right hand and made a stabbing motion.

Dante ignored him.

'He's in Y4,' Mr Cuddy told him. 'Get a move on.'

The cells in Corridor Y were reserved for patients who posed the highest level of risk. They had no windows, the bare minimum of furniture and an iron ring set in the wall to secure the chain to the patient's right leg. As Dante made his way up the metal staircase towards the patients' cells, he thought about the last time there had been an accident in the asylum. A patient called Gabriel had nearly strangled one of the doctors before he could be subdued by security staff. The doctor's throat had borne the marks of the man's fingers for weeks afterwards. Yet when Dante had brought him his food a few hours earlier, Gabriel had smiled sweetly and thanked him politely.

Keeble was on duty that morning. He was sitting on a stool underneath the huge portrait of Dr Sigmundus that hung above the entrance to each corridor. The doctor seemed to be frowning down on the security guard in disapproval. Perhaps this was not so surprising since Keeble was more easy-going than most. Unlike a lot of his colleagues, he was a man who enjoyed a chat with the other workers whenever he got the chance.

'Bit of a handful, this fellow,' he told Dante as he led the way along the corridor. 'If you ask me, they ought to have more than one of us on guard.' Seeing Dante's anxious face, he relented a little. 'Still, you needn't worry,' he went on, 'they took him straight to the Shock Room after admitting him. He won't be troubling anyone for a few hours.'

Dante was relieved to hear this. He'd seen patients after shock treatment. Most of them could scarcely move. They lay on their beds or sat on the floor staring vacantly, their mouths hanging open, dribbling saliva.

Keeble paused in front of the fourth cell. Then he took a huge collection of keys from his pocket and laboriously selected the right one. He opened the door and stepped aside to allow Dante to enter. It was the guard's job to open the door but he had to remain on the outside at all times, ready to shut and lock the door,

35

in case of any attempt to escape by the patient. If Dante was locked in the cell, then that was unfortunate but it was considered better than leaving the corridor unguarded.

Ezekiel Semiramis was slumped in a corner of the room, looking dazed and exhausted.

'I've brought you something to eat,' Dante told him, but there was no response.

He bent down and put the plate on the floor where it could be reached when the patient recovered. But he had made the mistake of coming too close. In an instant, Ezekiel Semiramis came to life. One hand seized Dante's right arm while the other clamped itself around his mouth.

'Don't struggle!' he hissed.

Dante did as he was instructed. The man was clearly much stronger than he looked, and all the stories Dante had heard about him came rushing into his head.

'Are you Dante?' Ezekiel Semiramis continued.

Dante could only nod in reply.

'Don't be frightened. I am not going to hurt you. I have something to tell you.'

Dante told himself that if he remained calm, the man would be more likely to release him.

'They told you your mother killed herself.'

This was the last thing that Dante had expected. How could this man know anything about his mother?

'Isn't that what they said?'

Dante nodded.

'It's a lie. She was murdered.'

Ezekiel Semiramis took his hand away from Dante's mouth and let go of his arm at the same time but Dante did not move. He was too shocked. He hadn't spoken about his mother to anyone for years. When he was younger some of the others had mocked him about her death. Jerome, in particular, used to enjoy asking him why he didn't jump out of the window like his mother. At first, this had reduced Dante to tears but in time he had learned to ignore it and Jerome had been forced to find new ways to insult him. But Dante had never really come to terms with the violence that had ended his mother's life and the mention of it now by a complete stranger bewildered him.

'How do you know about my mother?' he demanded.

'We were friends in the—' Ezekiel Semiramis began. But he stopped abruptly, as Keeble put his head around the door.

'What's going on here?' he demanded.

Ezekiel Semiramis picked up the plate and threw it against the wall. 'Take this filth away from me!' he shouted.

'That's enough!' Keeble told him, taking his truncheon out of its holder and brandishing it in Ezekiel's direction. 'You'll be back in the Shock Room if you carry on like that.' He turned to Dante. 'Come on. If he wants to go hungry, that's his choice.'

Dante picked up the tray and followed Keeble out of the room. 'Are you all right?' Keeble asked when he had locked the cell door.

'I'm fine,' Dante assured him.

'I think we're going to have a lot of trouble with that one,' Keeble said. 'I shouldn't go any closer to him than you have to. They say he's murdered dozens of people. The most dangerous patient we've ever had, that's what they reckon.'

Dante nodded but he wasn't really listening. As he made his way past the portrait of Dr Sigmundus and down the steps that led back to the kitchen, he thought about the prisoner's cryptic remarks. Perhaps they were simply the ravings of a madman. But how had Ezekiel known about his mother? On the other hand if it *were* true, what did it mean? Who would have murdered his mother? Why? And what else had Ezekiel been going to say before he had been interrupted?

The more Dante thought about it, the more he felt as if something inside him, something solid and hard that had been lodged in the centre of his being for as long as he could remember, was suddenly beginning to break apart. He stopped and clutched at the banister for support. He had known all sorts of pain – the ache of loneliness, the cuts and bruises that were the badges of bullying, the burns and scaldings that were part of a kitchen boy's lot – but he had never been hurt like this before. All he could do was try to catch his breath while he stood alone on the narrow metal stairs as hot tears ran down his cheeks.

THE RUINED CITY

It was very early in the morning. The sun had not yet risen above the clouds and a white mist hung over everything. Bea shivered and wrapped her arms around herself, trying to hug in the warmth of her body. She really should have worn a coat, she reflected. But it didn't matter. She was just so happy to be here. The others were still asleep. They would laugh when they heard she had been wandering through the empty streets at dawn but they would understand, for each one of them had known this feeling – a sense of freedom mingled with disbelief. Each one of them had felt the very same thing when they had first arrived.

A breeze sprang up from somewhere and the mist began to dissipate. Before her, Bea could see a set of cracked and broken steps that led to the front entrance of a huge building that was both strange and familiar. In the distance, a stone tower loomed out of the mist like an enormous finger pointing towards the sky. All around her, the once-magnificent architecture of the city was beginning to take shape, and Bea turned round slowly in a full circle to take it in.

'All this is mine,' she said out loud. Then she corrected herself. 'All this is ours.'

But even as she spoke, she was aware that something was starting to go wrong. The silence of the ruined streets was suddenly shattered by a harsh, unidentifiable noise. She covered her ears with her hands, but it made no difference. The noise continued with the unreasoning insistence of something mechanical. She wanted to cry out to her friends for help but they were oblivious to the unearthly clamour that grew louder by the second. She was certain that the moment of her death had come. Then with a sudden, fierce jolt, she woke.

She was in her bedroom in the asylum on Tarnagar. The alarm clock was bleeping. It was just another day.

As always when she woke from dreaming of the ruined city, Bea was left feeling bereft, like someone who has survived a great natural disaster that has swallowed up everyone else she knows. She lay in bed for a long time, trying desperately to cling to the exhilaration she had felt, the sense of purpose and belonging she had never experienced in her waking life. But the feelings drained away like water seeping through sand, and the memory of the dream disappeared with them until she could recall no more than the broken shapes of buildings and the stillness of empty streets.

When she went downstairs her mother and father were sitting at the kitchen table, their diaries in front of them, holding their usual Monday morning planning meeting. They scarcely looked up as she came into the room, helped herself to some cereal, and sat down at the end of the table.

'I've still got to finish collating the latest set of statistics in time for the quarterly report,' her father was saying.

'Does that mean you'll be working from home this week?' her mother asked.

'This week and next week. But only in the mornings. They're giving the new patient shock therapy in the afternoons, and I'll be assisting in the Recovery Room.'

Her mother nodded and made a note in her diary. 'You haven't forgotten that I'm carrying out assessments on Corridor Y this week, have you?' she continued.

Her father raised his eyebrows. 'Still working on Corridor Y? I thought you would have been finished there by now.'

'It's this whole business with the new patient. The administration department seems to have become completely flustered since they heard he was coming. We had to waste an entire afternoon reviewing security procedures. I don't know what they're so worried about.'

Bea allowed the rise and fall of her parents' voices to wash over her. A lot of the time, as long as she didn't draw attention to herself, they seemed to forget all about her.

She waited until her parents had closed their diaries, then she said, 'Why doesn't Ichor work on everyone?'

Her mother frowned and looked uncomfortable. She glanced at her husband, waiting to see how he would respond.

'It's an interesting question,' he said, 'and it shows

you're thinking about things, which is a good sign.'

'But it's best not to ask too many questions,' her mother added, smiling nervously. 'Everything will become clear in the fullness of time.'

Her father, who veered between being happy to answer questions on some days and completely outraged by them on others, was clearly in one of his more open-minded moods.

'No, no, Lucia,' he said, 'I think Bea's question deserves proper consideration.' He turned back to Bea. 'There have always been some poor individuals who are resistant to Ichor,' he told her. 'This was discovered a long time ago, when the decision was first made to give it to everyone. At first it was thought that something in the physical makeup of these people resisted the effect of the drug. Gradually, however, we learned that the problem was a mental one: what these sorry souls were suffering from was a disorder of the will. It was their minds, not their bodies that refused to co-operate. Not surprisingly, therefore, resistance to Ichor invariably goes hand-in-hand with a criminal personality. That is why our work in the clinic is about changing the patients' desires, so that they begin to want to be healthy.'

While Bea was listening to her father's explanation – and wondering whether or not it was true and if it was, how exactly Dante's criminal personality might manifest itself – Dante was bringing the inmates their breakfast.

He worked his way along each of the corridors in turn, beginning with the low-risk patients in Corridor A and ending with the handful of highly dangerous individuals in Corridor Y. Some of them spoke to him in a friendly manner; others regarded him with a hostile glare, as if they held him personally responsible for their incarceration. Until the previous day, however, none of them had ever laid a hand on him.

Despite his fear of what Ezekiel Semiramis was capable of, Dante was looking forward to bringing him his breakfast. Of course he might have nothing at all to say today. You never could tell; the behaviour of patients often changed dramatically from one day to the next. And perhaps there would be no opportunity for either of them to speak. A different guard would be on duty this morning and they were not all as relaxed as Keeble. Still, if the opportunity did arise and the man was willing to talk, then Dante was determined to find out more.

When he finally arrived on the landing of Corridor Y, McCluskey was pacing back and forth restlessly, his truncheon gripped firmly in one hand. Like many of the security staff, he sported a perfect replica of the bottlebrush moustache worn by Dr Sigmundus, and from time to time his free hand moved to his face, as if to check that it was still in place. McCluskey was Keeble's brother-in-law but, apart from the connection through marriage, the two men had nothing in common.

McCluskey looked irritably in Dante's direction. 'You're late,' he said.

'Problems in the kitchen,' Dante replied.

'Patients should be brought their meals on time,' McCluskey grumbled as he led the way down the corridor. 'Security's been getting very lax around here and it's going to have to be tightened up.'

Dante nodded. 'I'm sure you're right,' he said. Agreeing with McCluskey was always the easiest option.

There were only three other patients on Corridor Y: Salvador, Pavel, and the Snake Charmer. Salvador was Dante's favourite. He always gave Dante a big smile, regardless of what was on his plate, and he said the same thing every day: 'This looks really good.' Despite his pleasant manner, Dante was careful not to get too close. Salvador had been placed on Corridor Y after attacking one of the orderlies six months earlier. The man had suffered a broken nose and two cracked ribs in the assault.

In the next cell was Pavel. He was nearly seventy, with grey hair and a tremor in his hands; but he was still regarded as highly dangerous. A scar ran from his left eye down to his chin and one eye wandered restlessly in its socket, unable to focus, the result of a fight with another inmate years earlier. Some days he let out a string of curses whenever anyone entered the cell, but this morning he ignored Dante completely, merely sniffing loudly when the food was placed on the floor.

The Snake Charmer seemed the most harmless of the three. Dante had never heard of her being violent, though there must have been some sort of incident in the past, otherwise she would not have ended up on Corridor Y. She had been given her nickname because she was convinced that her cell was full of serpents. When her door was unlocked this morning and Dante stepped inside, she was sitting cross-legged on the bed, her long, grey hair hanging loosely down her back.

She held up her hand and pointed to the floor in front of him. 'Watch where you step,' she warned. 'There's more of them than usual today.'

Dante pretended to tread very carefully. He placed the food on the table beside the bed.

'I can't understand why there's so many,' the Snake Charmer told him.'

'Maybe it's a special day,' Dante suggested.

She looked at him eagerly. 'Do you think so?'

'I think it might be,' he told her, and she looked cheerful as he left and moved on to the next cell.

Just as on the previous day, Ezekiel Semiramis was slumped on the floor in a corner of his cell, as if scarcely conscious. But Dante was determined to stay at arm's length from him this time. He put the food down carefully on the floor and cautiously moved it closer with his foot.

The man sat up. 'What's the matter?' he asked. 'Scared?'

'Yes, I am,' Dante said, softly. 'I've heard about all the people you've killed.'

'Have you now?' An odd smile played across the patient's lips.

But Dante was determined not to be sidetracked. He

knew he only had a few seconds in which to find out the information he sought. 'You said you knew my mother,' he continued. 'How?'

'We were friends in the ruined city,' Ezekiel Semiramis told him.

Dante was taken aback. The ruined city rang a bell but he could not think where he had come across it before. Then he remembered Bea's drawing! He opened his mouth to ask more but there was no chance to speak as McCluskey appeared in the doorway.

'There's to be no fraternising with this patient,' he said, sharply.

Dante backed out of the room. All the way to the door, the piercing gaze of Ezekiel Semiramis followed him.

'What was he saying to you?' McCluskey asked when they were standing outside.

'Oh he was just complaining about the food,' Dante told him.

'He can count himself lucky,' McCluskey said. 'In a less generous society we wouldn't waste time keeping him alive at all. He'd have been executed the same day he was arrested.'

'I expect he would,' Dante agreed.

'He's got Dr Sigmundus to thank for the fact that he's still with us,' McCluskey went on, 'though I don't suppose he's grateful for it. If it was up to me, I wouldn't spend any more public money on him. You know what I'd do?'

'What?'

'Take him to the Shock Room and turn up the power.

Fry his brain. Call it an accident, if anyone wants to know. Who's going to worry if there's one less murderous loony to deal with?'

'I don't think that's a very good idea,' Dante said.

McCluskey looked at him sharply. 'What's the matter with you?' he demanded. He curled his lip in disgust. 'Oh yes, I forgot. Your mother was a loony, wasn't she?'

'I just do my job, Mr McCluskey,' Dante said. He turned and headed back down the stairs. He was not going to waste time arguing with McCluskey. If he could get the most important jobs out of the way quickly this morning, he might just have time to get to the school gates before the students arrived. And with a bit of luck, he might catch Bea before she went in. There were some questions he desperately needed to ask her.

RUMOURS

Dante put the wicker basket he was carrying on the floor and knocked loudly on the door of the laundry room. A few moments later the door opened and Polly's red-cheeked face peered out.

'Oh, it's you,' she said, dismissively. 'What do you want?'

'Mr Cuddy sent back these overalls,' Dante told her. 'He says they haven't been washed properly.'

'Not washed properly!' Polly said indignantly. She opened the lid of the basket and began dragging the overalls out to inspect them. 'They look perfectly clean to me.'

'Mr Cuddy's not happy with them,' Dante insisted. 'He says they need to be done again.'

Polly shook her head. 'I can't accept them,' she said, stuffing the overalls back in the basket. 'He'll have to take the matter up with Mrs Boxer.'

'Couldn't you just put them in the wash again without mentioning it to Mrs Boxer?' he pleaded.

'And why should I do that?' she demanded.

'It would make my life easier,' he said.

To his surprise, Polly's expression softened. 'All right then,' she said, 'I'll put them in myself. She'll never

48

know. But don't go telling anyone, or else they'll be wanting me to do it all the time.'

Dante looked at her with astonished gratitude. 'Thank you,' he said.

She shrugged. 'That's OK. Why don't you come in for a minute? Mrs Boxer's gone off to the pressing room and she won't be back for half an hour.'

Dante hesitated. He didn't have a lot of time, but he couldn't really refuse the invitation after Polly had gone out of her way to help him.

'Maybe just for a minute then,' he said.

Polly smiled, showing the small gap between her two front teeth. Nathaniel had once confessed that this imperfection made him go weak at the knees every time he saw it. Jerome had come back into the kitchen just at that moment and guffawed, declaring that in his opinion it made Polly look like a viper waiting to strike.

The laundry was dominated by a bank of huge washing machines. Whatever time of day or night you entered the room, the machines tumbled their contents round, hour after hour. The temperature in here was several degrees higher than anywhere else in the building, except perhaps the kitchen. Four young girls with their sleeves rolled up above their elbows and sweat running down their foreheads were busy putting dirty washing into the machines or taking clean washing out. They were known as loaders. Polly herself had started out as a loader but because of her ability she had risen to be Mrs Boxer's assistant.

As she led Dante across the room to the partitioned

area in the corner where Mrs Boxer had her office, one of the loaders approached her, a thin dark-haired girl with a limp.

'Number three machine's on the blink again, Polly,' she declared.

Polly nodded. 'You'd best report it to maintenance,' she told the girl, 'though I don't suppose they'll be able to do anything about it. Don't know why we bother with a maintenance department at all. Might as well give them all the sack and find them something useful to do.' She opened the door of the office. 'Come in and sit down,' she said to Dante. 'There's something I want to ask you.'

It was marginally quieter inside the office, and Dante sat down gratefully on a stool against the wall while Polly sat opposite him behind Mrs Boxer's desk. Dante wondered what Mrs Boxer would have to say if she knew that her assistant was taking liberties in her absence.

Polly wasted no time in getting down to business. 'I wanted to ask you about Nathaniel,' she told him.

'What about him?'

'Well, what's he like?'

'You know as well as I do what he's like,' Dante said.

Polly shook her head. 'But I don't,' she replied, 'leastways not the things that matter about him. Whereas you work with him.'

'Why me?' Dante asked, warily. 'Why don't you ask one of the others?'

Polly gave him another of her gap-toothed smiles.

'I reckon I can trust you,' she told him. 'You're not important enough to make trouble for anyone.'

'Thanks very much.'

'Come on,' Polly went on coaxingly, 'there's no need to get the hump. It's true, isn't it? No one bothers about what you think so you're in the best position to see things as they really are. So come on then, tell me what he's like.'

Dante shrugged. 'He's all right.'

'Is he hard working?'

'Reasonably.'

'Can he be relied on to do a thing if he says he will?'

'I think so.'

'Has he got a cruel streak?'

'No.'

'You're sure about that?'

'Yes.'

Polly nodded. 'Good. That's important.'

'Why do you want to know all this then?' Dante asked.

'Can't you guess?'

'Don't tell me he's finally plucked up the courage to pop the question?'

Polly smiled even wider than usual. 'That's right.'

'Well it took him long enough. He's been going on about you for as long as I can remember.'

'What does he say?'

'I think I'll let him tell you that.'

Polly looked disappointed but she soon perked up again. 'Maybe I should accept him then,' she said.

'What do you think?'

'Am I important enough to have an opinion about something like that?' Dante asked.

'Oh dear. Touchy, aren't we? Look, it's just a fact of life. You're a kitchen boy, and this being Tarnagar, there's not a lot you can do about it. Once upon a time things might have been different.'

'What do you mean?'

Polly leaned across the desk and lowered her voice. 'Well, I've heard that in the old days – before Dr Sigmundus came along, that is – where you stood in society didn't matter quite so much. Someone like me could have married anyone she wanted to – a senior doctor, or an administrator, or...' She struggled to think of a more elevated position than these. 'Well, anybody. Same with you. You wouldn't have had to stay a kitchen boy if you hadn't wanted to. Not if you'd had the ability to do better.'

'Who told you this?' Dante asked.

'My mother.'

'What does she know about it?'

'More than you think. She might have married a doctor, if things had been different.'

'What are you talking about?'

'My mother's a clever woman,' Polly told him. 'She's read books.'

'Your mother's a cleaner,' Dante pointed out. 'She works in the library. I've seen her.'

'That's what I'm saying, isn't it?' Polly went on. 'She works in the library because that's her station in life but if things were different she might have been somebody very grand. She's got the brains for it. Do you want to hear a secret?'

Dante hesitated. Although Polly had decided she could trust him, the feeling was not entirely mutual. She was the kind of girl to go around opening her mouth at the wrong time and getting other people into as much trouble as herself. However, she must have taken his lack of response as tacit agreement for she continued.

'When my mother was a young girl one of the doctors took a fancy to her.'

'What do you mean?'

'Well, he used to borrow library books for her and they would talk about them together. Of course, they got found out and that put an end to their romance – you know what Tarnagar's like. But what I'm saying is this: my mother knows a thing or two and she told me that our society wasn't always so rigid. Once upon a time you could rise to the level of your ability.'

'I don't see that it makes much difference to us, though,' Dante said. 'I'm going to stay a kitchen boy whatever I do, and you're still going to marry Nathaniel.'

'Here! I haven't said I will marry him yet,' Polly objected. 'I shall have to think about it, so don't you go telling him any different.'

'I won't say a word,' Dante told her.

Polly opened her mouth to say something more but the office door suddenly opened and the girl with the limp put her head inside.

'Mrs Boxer's at the end of the corridor,' she hissed. 'Angie saw her when she went out for more soap powder.'

'Thanks Fritha,' Polly said. She got up quickly and propelled Dante outside. 'You'd best go out the back door,' she told him, 'otherwise she'll want to know what you've been doing here.'

Dante nodded.

'And you won't breathe a word of what I said to anyone, will you?' she went on, as she hurried him across the room.

''Course not.'

'I knew I could trust you.'

As Dante was leaving the laundry behind, Bea was making her way to school in the company of Francesca Belmonti, who was keen to hear her opinion on a subject of the greatest importance.

'Tamsin Rivoli says that Edmund Dubrovnik told her that I was the most fascinating girl he'd ever encountered,' she informed Bea. 'Those were his actual words – the most fascinating girl he'd ever encountered. And she said that he really wanted to ask me out, but he was too shy to do it himself so he asked her to ask me for him. What do you think I should say?'

This was the third time Francesca had posed the very same question, and it was all Bea could do to keep from screaming. Edmund Dubrovnik was a thoroughly boring boy in the year above them. He was reasonably good-looking, but he had bad dandruff and the most stuck-up voice Bea had ever heard. However, his father was a senior doctor, which was why Francesca was so excited about the whole thing. If his father had been a cleaner, she would be marvelling at his cheek.

Bea had hoped that by simply ignoring Francesca's dilemma, she might be allowed to continue on her way to school in peace but Francesca was not prepared to drop the subject until she got a satisfactory response.

'Out where?' Bea finally replied.

Francesca looked confused. 'Whatever do you mean?' she demanded.

'You said he wants to ask you out. Out where exactly? I mean, where is there to go on Tarnagar?'

'Oh for heaven's sake, Bea, it's just a manner of speaking,' Francesca said petulantly. 'There's no need to take it literally. The important question is, should I accept?'

'Well you obviously want to.'

'Yes, but I don't want to appear too keen.'

'Then say no.'

A murmur of exasperation escaped from between Francesca's lips. 'Really Bea, you aren't being very helpful,' she said.

'It's not the sort of thing I know anything about,' Bea told her.

'Well perhaps it's time you started to think about it,' Francesca suggested, putting on her most matronly voice. 'After all, we've both got our coming-of-age ceremonies in a few weeks, haven't we?'

'What's that got to do with it?'

Francesca's face took on a similar expression to Bea's mother's when she thought Bea was being deliberately difficult. 'It means we're getting to the age where boys can't be ignored anymore. They're a factor that has to be taken into consideration.'

'Not by me,' Bea told her.

'You'll change your mind,' Francesca insisted, smugly.

'I'm not the sort of person who changes her mind. Besides, all the boys I know are far too interested in themselves to waste their time on me.'

Francesca sighed. 'I think you behave like this on purpose,' she said.

'Behave like what?'

'As if you don't understand the simplest things.'

They had arrived at the school gates by now. A number of students were standing around in little knots, waiting until the last minute before going inside. A group of girls called out greetings to Francesca, and she went over to speak to them. Bea walked towards the entrance, relieved to be by herself. Suddenly, she heard someone call her name and, looking up, saw Dante making his way over to join her.

She was so startled to see him that she simply stared in confusion while he mumbled something incomprehensible about a new patient who had been admitted to the clinic. Bea vaguely remembered her father saying something about the same man at the breakfast table, but why Dante had come to the school to tell her this news was quite beyond her. Perhaps he really was mentally unbalanced. With a sense of growing anxiety, she recalled her father's opinion about resistance to Ichor. She glanced over to where Francesca and her friends were standing and, with a sinking heart, saw that they were staring at her.

When she turned back to Dante, he seemed to be undoing the buttons of his shirt. At first she began to panic. But then she saw that he was taking out something that he had been keeping inside it. It was a drawing, her drawing of the ruined city.

'Where did you get that?' she demanded.

'I found it on the ground after you left, yesterday,' he told her. 'I think you must have dropped it.'

'Oh. Well, thank you,' Bea said. She quickly took the drawing from him and stuffed it into her school bag.

'That's why I need to talk to you,' Dante went on. 'I have to find out about this place in the drawing.'

Bea started to pay attention. 'What do you know about the ruined city?' she asked.

'Nothing,' he said, 'except that my mother once lived there – at least that's what Ezekiel Semiramis told me.'

Just then the school bell began to ring. 'Look, I can't discuss this now,' Bea whispered. 'I have to go into school.'

'Can I meet you this evening, then?' Dante asked.

Bea hesitated. What if Dante could throw some light on her dreams?

'Where do you want to meet?' she asked.

'In the woods. At seven o'clock. The same place we met before.'

'All right.'

It was only after he had slipped away that Bea realised what she had done. If her parents found out, there would be terrible trouble.

As she was thinking this, she was joined by Francesca and her friends, looking highly amused.

'Well, well, well,' Francesca said. 'Beatrice Argenti, who would have believed it? Fancy you making out that you were such a goody-goody all this time.'

'I don't know what you're talking about.'

Francesca shook her head in mock amazement. 'A kitchen boy!' she said. 'No wonder you've been keeping quiet about it. That's something to be ashamed of, all right.' Then she brushed past Bea with her nose in the air, closely followed by the other girls.

Bea sighed. There was no point in trying to defend herself. It was obvious from the looks on her classmates' faces that they had found something that would keep them entertained for some time.

Mr Cuddy, the catering manager, had always been on the heavy side. Jerome referred to him as 'that old walrus', though never, of course, within his hearing. Mr Cuddy's plump face was generally flushed pink with the exertion of scuttling about the corridors of the asylum trying to make sure the complicated business of feeding staff and inmates was running smoothly. This morning, however, as Dante stepped inside the kitchen door, the catering manager's complexion was the colour of beetroot and beads of sweat glistened between the furrows on his forehead.

'Where the hell have you been?' he demanded.

Dante knew he was in serious trouble. This called for quick thinking.

'I had to go on an errand for Mrs Boxer,' he began, but before he could go any further, Mr Cuddy struck him on the side of the head.

'Liar!' he shouted. 'I spoke to Mrs Boxer just five minutes ago. She had no idea where you were. Tell the truth. You were skiving, weren't you?'

'No, sir,' Dante replied. 'I was—' But another blow to the other side of the head cut him short again.

'You are a lazy, idle, ungrateful and deceitful boy,'

Mr Cuddy told him. 'We would all be much better off without you.' He took hold of Dante's ear between two of his podgy fingers and twisted it viciously. 'Do you know what I will do if I ever catch you skiving again?' he demanded.

'No, sir.' Forced up onto his toes by the pain in his ear, Dante was thinking that he would very much like to punch Mr Cuddy as hard as he could in that great, fat gut. He could just picture the catering manager doubling up in pain. But he knew that if he so much as raised one finger against his tormentor, or indeed against anyone in the kitchen, he would soon be sitting in a cell, chained to the wall.

'I'll take a strap to you,' Mr Cuddy continued. 'And I'll leather you within an inch of your life. Do I make myself clear?'

'Yes, sir.'

Reluctantly, Mr Cuddy released him. 'Bad blood always shows itself in the end,' he said.

'Will that be all, sir?' Dante asked, nursing his throbbing ear.

'No it will not be all,' Mr Cuddy told him. 'In fact I rather think that it's just the beginning for you, young man. I don't know what you've been up to this time but the director wants to see you, right away.'

'The director?' Dante repeated in disbelief.

'That's what I said,' Mr Cuddy snapped. 'And you'd better make your way to his office pretty smartly because he's not a man who likes to be kept waiting.'

Dante had never heard of anyone being summoned

to Mr Appollyon's office before. In fact, he had only seen the director once, when an important official had come from the mainland to inspect the clinic and everyone had gathered near the entrance to watch his arrival. Even then he had only caught a brief glimpse of a tall, rather distinguished-looking figure greeting his guest with a great deal of bowing and shaking of hands.

As Dante made his way along the corridors towards the Administration Block, he racked his brains but he could think of no offence serious enough to be worthy of the director's personal attention. He could only conclude that the decision he had long feared had finally been taken: they were going to declare him a patient and lock him away. He began to feel physically sick.

Once he had passed through the double doors that connected the Domestic Block with the Administration Block, his surroundings changed dramatically. Unlike the corridors in Dante's part of the asylum, these were carpeted, and whereas the only decoration in the Domestic Block had been the portraits of Dr Sigmundus above every door, here the walls were hung with framed pictures at regular intervals, scenes from nature mostly – peaceful landscapes with rolling countryside, winding rivers and distant hills.

At last he reached the section in which the director's office was located. A sign on the wall warned him that this area was reserved for senior members of the administration and that any other personnel were admitted only by appointment. At the very end of the corridor was an imposing oak door that bore on its front a brass nameplate inscribed with the words, 'Leopold Appollyon, Asylum Director'.

Dante hesitated, then summoning up all his courage, he knocked on the door.

'Come in,' a woman's voice called.

Mr Appollyon's secretary glanced up as Dante opened the door. She looked him up and down dismissively. 'Did you want something?' she said.

'Mr Appollyon asked to see me,' Dante mumbled.

'Speak up please.'

'Mr Appollyon asked to see me.'

'And your name is?'

'Dante Cazabon.'

'I'll tell him you're here.'

She got up from her desk, went over to a door at the other end of the room and knocked. Then she disappeared inside. While he waited, Dante looked around the room. He wondered whether any of the documents piled on the desk referred to him, but since he could not read, there was no point in trying to steal a look. Instead, he shifted nervously from foot to foot, until the door at the far end of the room opened again and the secretary re-emerged.

'Mr Appollyon will see you right away,' she told him. 'Just go straight through.'

Dante opened the door and stepped inside. Mr Appollyon's office was at least four times the size of the one his secretary occupied. It was dominated by a huge window along one wall. Mr Appollyon was sitting behind a large mahogany desk, gazing out of that window, and ignoring Dante completely. At last, however, he turned and considered his visitor.

'So you're the kitchen boy,' he said, speaking almost too quietly for Dante to hear.

'Yes, sir.'

There was an empty chair facing the desk, but Mr Appollyon did not invite Dante to sit. Instead he clasped his fingers together, and swivelled gently from side to side in his chair. His face looked haggard and there were deep shadows under his eyes, as if he had not slept properly in a long time. For some while he continued to regard Dante in silence, as though considering a specimen in a glass case. Finally he spoke.

'You've been bringing the new patient, Ezekiel Semiramis, his meals, I understand?'

'Yes, sir.'

'And I'm told by the security staff that you engaged in conversation with him yesterday?'

'No, sir.'

Mr Appollyon sighed. 'Please don't waste my time.'

'I'm sorry, sir,' Dante told him. 'It's just that we didn't engage in conversation – at least, not really.'

'Not really? Just what is that supposed to mean?'

'Well, he asked me why the food was so cold and I said that it was nothing to do with me. I just bring it up from the kitchen.'

'And you're telling me that's all that was said?'

'Yes, sir.'

Mr Appollyon shook his head. 'I'm not sure I believe you.'

'It's the truth, sir,' Dante assured him, trying his hardest to sound convincing.

There was another long pause. Then Mr Appollyon seemed to come to a decision. 'You are not to bring the prisoner his meals again,' he said. 'I will make arrangements for one of the security staff to come down to the kitchen and collect them. That will be all.'

Dante nodded. 'Thank you, sir.' He turned to go but before he could do so Mr Appollyon spoke again.

'I'll be watching you from now on, Dante Cazabon. Do you understand?'

'Yes, sir.'

'Good. I like people to understand me.' He spoke very softly, but there was no mistaking the menace in his voice.

A DIFFICULT CONVERSATION

It didn't take long for word to get round. By the middle
of the day every girl in Bea's class, and most of the boys
too, had heard that Beatrice Argenti was going out with
a kitchen boy. By lunchtime she was completely
ostracised. No one would talk to her, no one would even
sit at the same table as her. Instead, they gathered in
little groups, avidly gossiping. Everyone agreed that it
was the most appalling thing they'd ever heard but, at
the same time, it was just what you might expect from
Beatrice. She always wanted to be different. Well, she
had certainly proved that now. But a kitchen boy! How
could she? One thing was certain: no boy was going to
be interested in her now. She was tarnished. That was
the only word for it.

Poor thing, some of the kinder ones said, but
Francesca Belmonti did not agree. 'She's had this coming
to her for a long time,' she told them. 'I've tried to talk to
her but she just wouldn't listen. She thought she was
above the rest of us. Well, there are certain things that
simply aren't done and I'm afraid she's going to have to
learn that the hard way.'

The others all nodded sagely. They knew that
Francesca was right and even if some of them did feel

a bit sorry for Bea, no one was going to get up, walk across the dining hall and sit down beside her. That would have been social suicide.

The boys were even worse – pointing in Bea's direction and sniggering. Whenever she came within hearing distance they called out insults. 'Desperate' or 'skivvy-lover' were two of their favourites. Edmund Dubrovnik came up to Bea outside the dining room and asked her what she thought of the food.

Bea looked at him in confusion.

'If you ask me it's absolutely disgraceful,' he said. 'I was thinking of making an official complaint but I wasn't sure who to talk to. Then I thought – with your connections in the kitchen you must know exactly who I need to speak to.'

There were howls of laughter from his cronies as he said this.

'Hilarious,' Bea told him.

Wherever she went, people moved away from her as if she had some dreadful disease. I hate this place, she thought to herself while she sat alone picking at her lunch. If I ever get the chance, I'm going to leave here and never come back.

But she would not be allowed to leave the island until she was eighteen and only then to study medicine. Given her family background, the authorities would be unlikely to approve any other course. When her time at university was over she would be obliged to come back to the asylum and work on Tarnagar. That was her life and it was how things would remain.

Of course she really ought to go to Francesca and confide in her. That was what Francesca wanted and it was Bea's reluctance to do so in the past that had made Francesca so spiteful. But if she did that, Bea would have to explain about wandering in the woods by herself, which Francesca would consider a very odd thing to do. Then she would have to explain about meeting Dante and having a conversation with him about dreams. Francesca would be appalled; she would say that of course Bea should have ignored him completely. Finally, she would have to explain about the ruined city. And how on earth could she do that? Francesca would probably feel it was her duty to go off immediately and inform someone in authority.

Bea couldn't really blame her. She didn't even understand what was happening, herself. Why did she keep dreaming about the ruined city? And how was it that Dante seemed to know something about the place? Hadn't he said that his mother had lived there? Well there was only one way to find out. Even if everyone who knew her thought that she was crazy or sick or even perverted, she would have to talk to him.

In the afternoon Bea's class had a double lesson of history. They were studying the events that had led up to the Establishment of Permanent Peace. Mr Samphire, the head of history, was a little man who talked through his nose in a way that made him sound as if he always had a cold. He would have been utterly forgettable had he not chosen to wear the largest and ugliest pair of glasses anyone had ever seen.

67

'As you are all aware,' Mr Samphire was saying, 'the period before the Establishment of Permanent Peace was one of the most dreadful eras in human history. Society was ravaged by crime. It wasn't safe to walk the streets. Murder and robbery were everyday occurrences. And on the international stage it was just the same: nation fought against nation for the most trivial of reasons. All around the world countries descended into chaos and barbarism. Only in Gehenna was civilisation preserved, thanks to the wisdom and foresight of one man, Dr Stanislaus Sigmundus.'

Mr Samphire pulled down a chart at the front of the room. It showed Gehenna surrounded by sea on all sides except to the north where Tavor lay just across the mountains. He pointed out Tarnagar, their island, lying just off the most southerly point. Both Tarnagar and Gehenna were drawn in green, to show they existed in a state of peace and harmony. Whereas Tavor, and the countries beyond, where people were no better than barbarians, were coloured red, signifying violence and lawlessness. But Bea had stopped paying attention. She was thinking about the ruined city. Recently, whenever she woke up from one of her dreams, she retained a distinct feeling that there had been other people in the dream: companions. No, more than that: friends.

Friends! The very thought of the word made her ache inside. It was what she missed most of all when she woke up, the sense that there were others who thought like her. She could feel tears coming into her eyes and she hurriedly blinked them back. Never, in all her life on Tarnagar, had there been anyone whom she could really call a friend. The girls and boys with whom she had grown up had all been like Francesca Belmonti, the kind of people who would be only too happy to spread ugly rumours about you, if they could just discover something colourful enough to make it worth their while. Now Francesca had as juicy a piece of gossip as she was ever likely to get, and she was clearly determined to make the most of it.

'Perhaps you can tell us the answer, Beatrice, 'Mr Samphire suggested, his nasal voice cutting abruptly into her daydream. She looked up in dismay, aware that everyone in the classroom was staring at her with amused expectation.

'Could you repeat the question please, sir?' she asked.

'You would know what the question was if you had been paying attention,' he pointed out.

'She's got other things to think about, sir,' Francesca volunteered.

'She's dreaming about being a kitchen maid,' one of the other girls added. The rest of the class tittered.

'All right, that will do,' Mr Samphire told them. 'The question, Beatrice, was how did Dr Sigmundus begin the famous speech in which he announced the beginning of the coming-of-age ceremony. Can anyone tell me?'

Francesca Belmonti's hand shot up.

'Yes, Francesca?'

'"My fellow citizens, I am proud to announce that the

war against crime has finally been won."'

'Splendid, Francesca. Gold star. Now do try to pay attention in future, Beatrice.'

'Yes, sir.'

As Mr Samphire continued to extol the virtues of Dr Sigmundus – his wisdom, his far-sightedness and his dedication to the good of all humanity – Bea found herself thinking that human beings must have been very nasty indeed before the introduction of Ichor.

'Going off to meet your kitchen boy?' Araminta McCracken called, as Bea tried to hurry away unnoticed when it was time to go home. Araminta was usually the subject of other girls' taunts because of a dark red birthmark on the left side of her neck. She seemed delighted that someone else had taken over her position.

Bea sighed and walked away as quickly as she could. Neither of her parents was at home when she got back, so she decided to do her homework. She had not completely made up her mind yet whether she really was going to meet Dante but she wanted to make sure that if she did decide to do so, there would be nothing to prevent her. While she was sitting at the kitchen table, looking at the essay Mr Samphire had set the class, a scratching noise at the door announced that Nelson wanted to come in.

Nelson was her cat. He had been given to her for her fourth birthday and she had originally called him Nellie because she had been under the impression that he was female.

She got up and opened the door. Nelson immediately

came running in, and she saw that he had a mouse in his mouth.

'Oh, Nelson!' she shrieked. 'Get that out of here!'

Nelson ran under the table and crouched there eyeing her suspiciously, the mouse still dangling from his mouth. Then, to Bea's horror, he opened his mouth to meow and in the process managed to drop the mouse, which she now saw was alive. It made a feeble attempt to escape but Nelson's paw came down upon it immediately, stopping it in its tracks. He seized it between his jaws again.

Bea picked up the kitchen broom and pushed it under the table towards him. 'Get out, Nelson!' she shouted.

Nelson scampered out from under the table, and she chased him out of the room, slamming the door shut behind him. Then she sat down at the table and tried to go on with her homework, but it was difficult. She kept thinking of the poor mouse. After a while she got up and went over to the window. Nelson was just outside, on the patio. She had expected him to have eaten the mouse by now but to her surprise it was still in his mouth. As she watched, he dropped it again. Just as before, the mouse made a pathetic attempt to escape but it did not get far before Nelson's paw pinned it to the ground. She watched as this process was repeated several times and gradually it dawned on her that Nelson was playing with the mouse, extending the process of killing it in order to extract as much satisfaction as possible from the game.

'What a horrible animal you are, Nelson!' she said.

And yet he was always so cute and cuddly when he wanted feeding.

When her mother came home a little while later, Bea told her about what she had seen. Her mother was unperturbed.

'It's just his nature,' she said. 'Cats are natural hunters.'

'But he doesn't need to hunt for food,' Bea pointed out. 'He gets plenty to eat from us.'

Her mother shrugged. 'It's his instinct,' she replied. 'It doesn't matter how much we feed him, he still likes to kill.'

'Well I don't like him,' Bea declared.

'I don't suppose that bothers him greatly,' her mother said.

But Bea found it more difficult to dismiss Nelson's behaviour. She wondered why this was, why she should be so upset about a mouse, which she certainly wouldn't want in the house. Maybe it was because the creature was trying so hard to get away.

She considered telling her father about it when he came back a little later that evening, but he was no longer in the good mood he had displayed at breakfast. One of his colleagues had made an error at work and he had been blamed. It was something very minor to do with the collection of statistics but he complained bitterly as he went around the house, banging doors and muttering to himself. It was this, as much as anything else, that made Bea decide she would meet Dante as they had agreed. At least she would be out of the house, away from her mother's indifference and her father's bad temper.

After dinner, she announced that she was going over to see Francesca. Her mother looked pleased. She considered Francesca a very good influence on Bea.

'You two must have so much to talk about,' she said happily, 'what with your coming-of-age ceremonies being on the same day.'

Bea just nodded. She could not bring herself to agree.

'Well don't get over-excited,' her mother went on. 'There's still a few weeks to go.'

'I'll try not to,' Bea said.

It wasn't difficult to make her way down to the woods without anyone seeing her. There were never many people about in the evenings. Tarnagar was a very predictable place. People got up in the morning, went to school or else to work, came home in the evening, had their dinner, did a few chores and went to bed. Going out after dusk was discouraged.

Once Bea had crossed the lawn and entered the woods, it seemed as if she had completely left behind the person her parents expected her to be. In among the trees the light was gloomier and the air seemed thicker. The carpet of leaves underfoot deadened all sound and she felt like some wild creature, prowling through the twilight.

She found Dante waiting where they had parted the previous week. He thanked her for coming and then began to explain what it was all about. He went more slowly this time, starting with the story of his mother's death, then telling her what Ezekiel Semiramis had said and finally describing his interview with the director.

'Why do you think Mr Appollyon was so keen to make sure you didn't speak to Ezekiel Semiramis?' she asked.

'I don't know,' Dante said. 'I suppose it could be that he's such a security risk they don't want him talking to anyone, but on the other hand it might be because they're worried he'll tell me something they don't want me to know. That's why I need to find out what you know about this ruined city.'

He was looking at her so earnestly that Bea hated to disappoint him, but she could only tell the truth.

'I don't know anything about it,' she said.

He looked dismayed. 'You must! What about your drawing?'

This was going to be difficult. Bea knew perfectly well that a girl who had been properly brought up did not talk about her dreams. It simply wasn't done. But Dante didn't seem to understand that.

'I can't explain,' she told him.

Now his dismay turned to confusion. 'Why not?'

She hated having to conceal something from him but this was so awkward. How could she let him know, without actually spelling it out? Then she had an idea.

'Listen, last time we met, you told me a secret,' she began.

'You mean about Ichor not working on me?'

'Yes and I asked you how you knew. Do you remember what you told me?'

He thought for a moment. 'That I still had dreams?'

Bea nodded. 'Yes.'

He waited for her to carry on but she just looked meaningfully at him. 'I don't understand,' he said.

Bea could feel her face growing hot with embarrassment. Why couldn't he make the connection?

'That's how I know about the ruined city,' she told him. 'The same way that you know Ichor doesn't work on you.'

He frowned. 'You mean you dream about it?'

'Yes.'

'Well why didn't you say so?'

'It's not the sort of thing you're supposed to talk about.'

Dante was silent for a little while. Then he said, 'Haven't you ever wondered about that? I mean why aren't we supposed to talk about our dreams? What's so bad about that?'

Bea was feeling increasingly uncomfortable. One part of her was telling her that she ought to turn round and go home now. Maybe her father was right. Dante obviously felt no compunction about ignoring the rules of polite society. So there was no telling what he might do next. But another part of her kept insisting that he was not a threat, that he was only saying out loud the sorts of things she had been thinking for a very long time. And that other part of her was longing to trust someone with the secrets she had been storing up inside herself.

'Look,' Dante said. 'I know this is difficult for you and, if you like, we can both go home now and forget this whole conversation. I promise I will never mention it to another soul. But before we do that, let's just look at the alternative. OK?'

Bea nodded. 'OK.'

'Right. Well, I think you really want to tell someone about your dreams and I really need to hear about them. So we've both got something to gain, haven't we? All you need to do is trust me. It's up to you.'

It was the first time in her life that Bea had been asked to make a real decision. Everything else had always been decided for her by her parents or her teachers. She looked at Dante, waiting for him to try to persuade her, but he remained silent. In the end, it was that quiet determination not to interfere that made up her mind.

'All right then,' she said. 'I'll tell you. But there isn't much to tell.'

She described as much as she could remember of her dreams and he listened without interrupting. Once she'd overcome her initial embarrassment, she felt a huge sense of relief as she told him about the sense of friendship she encountered and the feeling of bereavement she experienced on waking.

'How many times have you had the dream?' Dante asked.

'I haven't counted,' she told him. 'Ten or twelve times, I suppose.'

'It's got to mean something.'

'Yes but what?'

Dante shrugged.

'Do you think there really is such a place?' Bea went on.

'Ezekiel Semiramis seemed to think so.'

'He's insane, remember? That's why he's here.'

Dante looked dubious. 'He didn't seem insane to me.'

'That doesn't mean a thing. My father told me that people can seem completely normal on the surface but underneath they can be quite mad.'

'Your father would probably think the same thing about me.'

His suggestion was so accurate that Bea couldn't think of a reply.

'I'm right, aren't I?' Dante asked.

'Yes. I'm sorry.'

'Don't worry about it. I'm used to it. All my life people have been telling me that my mother was a loony and they've been waiting for me to turn out the same way. That's why I need to know the truth about her death.'

'I wish I could do more to help,' Bea said.

'You've done as much as you can,' Dante told her. 'What I really need is a chance to talk to Ezekiel Semiramis properly. But that's not going to happen now. Mr Appollyon's made sure of that.'

'Look, I'm going to have to go in a minute,' Bea said, 'otherwise my parents will start wondering where I am.'

Dante nodded.

Bea hesitated. There was something else she needed to say to him but she had to be careful about saying it.

'If you want to speak to me again,' she told him, 'it's probably best if you don't come to the school. It's just that, well, you know what Tarnagar is like. Everyone notices everything.'

'I suppose it must have made things difficult for you when I turned up like that,' Dante said. 'I was just so excited that I had to talk to you.'

'It doesn't matter,' Bea said. 'But I think it's wiser if we keep any other meetings to ourselves.' She thought for a minute. 'I know,' she said. 'There's a hole in the base of this tree.' She bent down to show him and he saw that where the trunk of the tree met the ground there was a hollow that went right back into the tree. 'We could write notes and leave them here,' she said eagerly.

Dante gave her an odd look. 'I don't think that's a very good idea.'

'Why not? No one's going to see if we cover them up with leaves. I've got a little wooden box that my parents gave me when I was a child. We could use that to put them in.'

'It wouldn't work,' Dante insisted.

'What's wrong with it?'

'I can't read,'

'You can't read?'

'You wouldn't be able to either if you'd never been to school.'

'But why didn't you go to school?'

'Because I'm not important enough,' he told her bitterly. 'I'm nobody.'

'I'm sorry,' Bea said. 'I didn't realise.'

'It doesn't matter.'

She could see that it did matter but could think of no

way to make up for her blunder. Then she had an idea.

'Have you got a handkerchief?'

Dante shook his head.

Bea took hers out of her pocket and held it out. 'Here, have mine,' she told him. 'If you need to talk to me about something, put it in the tree, and pile a lot of leaves on top of it. If I find it, I'll come here at this time on the same day. If I want to speak to you, I'll do the same..

Dante hesitated.

'It's better than leaving a note,' Bea went on, 'because even if someone finds it, there's nothing that traces it to us.'

'All right.' He put the handkerchief in his pocket.

'I'd better go,' Bea said.

'Thanks for coming.'

'That's OK.'

They stood there slightly awkwardly for a moment. Then Bea turned and walked away. Her stride was purposeful and determined and yet she was so slight that seen from behind she could have been a much younger girl. Dante watched until she was out of sight. Then he took the handkerchief from his pocket and held it in his hand, feeling the softness of the material between his finger and thumb.

RELICS

Tuesday afternoon was devoted to preparation classes for students whose coming-of-age ceremonies were due within the next two months. There were ten of them altogether, including Beatrice and Francesca. Their ceremonies were scheduled to take place over two weekends. Each person's ceremony would be conducted separately, of course, though, as Miss Flambard informed them, things had been done differently when the coming-of-age ritual was first introduced. In those days group ceremonies had been the norm. She was standing in the centre of the Dagabo as she said this, where the adults all went to receive Ichor once a week. To one side of the dispensing table stood a large jug of water, a number of small tumblers and a plate of sweets. In the middle of the table was a small, golden box – the reliquary.

'Nowadays, we have come to realise that the ceremony is too important to be shared with others,' she said in her high-pitched, fluty voice. 'It's a very special moment in the life of each boy and girl and the individual ceremony acknowledges that.'

Miss Flambard was commonly referred to by the students as Miss Flamingo, since her neck seemed far too long for the rest of her body. Bea liked to imagine that one day she might suddenly sprout wings and take off. Sadly, Miss Flambard was really a very ordinary person and never likely to do anything quite so remarkable.

She was about fifty years of age, very thin and pale and known to live by herself, a circumstance that made her an object of the greatest scorn among the inhabitants of Tarnagar. As far as they were concerned, the failure to make a good marriage was a shameful thing. It was not that they placed great store by love. Indeed, love, in the abstract, was almost never mentioned by anyone. No, it was allying yourself with another family of equal, or preferably, greater rank that mattered. Cementing your importance and the importance of your family. Remaining single meant getting left out and it was never a good idea to be left out of anything. You did not want to become an oddball, a loner, someone who didn't fit in – someone like Beatrice Argenti.

None of them was sitting anywhere near her but she didn't mind so much here in the Dagabo where there was plenty of room for everyone to spread out. While Miss Flambard continued with her lecture about the development of the coming-of-age ceremonies, Bea felt free to daydream. She was not likely to be asked any difficult questions today. Miss Flambard was not the kind of teacher who sought out confrontation. It would probably never even occur to her that one of her students might not be paying attention to a talk about their impending coming-of-age ceremony. It was the most important day in a person's life, after all. Surely everyone would want to know as much about it as possible? To savour every minute of anticipation and preparation?

Miss Flambard moved on to consider the construction of the Dagabo itself. 'Every Dagabo is built to exactly the same design,' she told them, 'and all over this wonderful country of ours boys and girls exactly like you are going through precisely the same ritual. I know that you will find this a reassuring thought.'

She pointed to the doorway through which they had all entered earlier that afternoon. 'The twin pillars of the Newcomers' Entrance which you all passed through on your way to today's lesson symbolise the two most important responsibilities of adulthood: duty and achievement. And, as I'm sure you're all aware, there are fourteen steps leading up to those pillars, one step for each year of your life so far. When the great day arrives, the seats you are sitting in now will be filled with your family, your friends and the teachers who have watched over your progress in your journey through life so far. The official recorder will be standing exactly where I am now and as you cross the threshold, he will call out your name and welcome you to the adult world.'

Miss Flambard smiled broadly. 'I can assure you, it is a moment you will remember all your lives.' There was a faraway look in her eyes as she said this, as if she were recalling her own coming-of-age. Ordinarily, such a display of sentiment would have provoked a cynical response from the students. Someone would have made a facetious comment or a crude gesture that would have caused the others to erupt into laughter. But this time Bea could see that they were listening with rapt attention. For a moment she envied the others, wishing she could suspend the little voice inside her head that kept on questioning everything.

'In a minute we're going to practise the ritual itself,' Miss Flambard continued, 'but before we do that, I want to draw your attention to the reliquary.'

Ten pairs of eyes swivelled obediently to the little box covered with gold leaf and studded with precious stones that stood in the middle of the dispensing table. 'As you know,' Miss Flambard continued, 'every Dagabo contains a reliquary at its heart. It's a great honour that Dr Sigmundus has granted to his people. The gift of himself – that is how he asks us to think of it. And the fact that he has placed that gift here, in the Dagabo, where every citizen over fourteen years of age comes once a week to receive Ichor, shows us how important these rituals are to the life of our society.

'What you may not know, however, is that there are degrees of importance among reliquaries. The least important hold nothing more than a fragment of cloth that Dr Sigmundus has held in his hands. I say nothing more, though of course that in itself is something very special. However, there are some reliquaries that Dr Sigmundus considers so significant, so essential to the life of our community, that he has allowed something that is truly a part of himself to be placed within them.'

Miss Flambard paused. She knew that she held her audience in the palm of her hand now. She leaned towards them, her voice reverent. 'The reliquary of Tarnagar contains some of Dr Sigmundus's own hair,' she whispered.

Bea didn't know whether she felt more like shuddering or laughing out loud. Luckily she had the good sense to do neither. Looking round at the rest of the audience, she could see they had received this news in the same respectful manner that Miss Flambard had delivered it. They felt deeply honoured. Bea could sense the warm glow of that honour spreading throughout the Dagabo, cheering everyone who sat within its precinct, all but one.

'Why has Dr Sigmundus chosen to favour our little community in this way?' Miss Flambard continued. 'Why this special privilege for Tarnagar? It is because of the work we do here, the work that your mothers and fathers are engaged in every day and in which you will one day play your part. Some people think that Tarnagar is a little backwater, an isolated place, cut off from the mainstream of society. Well those people could not be more wrong. Those of us who live and work in the asylum are the guardians of society – and that is something you must never forget.'

All around her, Bea could see heads nodding in agreement.

'Now then,' Miss Flambard went on. 'It's time for our little rehearsal. Can you all line up at the back beside the two pillars, in alphabetical order.'

Bea realised, with a sinking feeling, that she would be first in the queue.

'Right then,' Miss Flambard continued when they had all taken their positions. 'I shall take the part of the Official Recorder and call out your names. Beatrice Argenti, step forward.'

Bea walked up the central aisle towards the dispensing table, stopping at the point where a golden star had been painted on the floor.

'Why have you come to the Dagabo?' Miss Flambard intoned, her voice pitched several tones lower than usual.

'I have come to receive the gift of Ichor which has been granted to us by our great benefactor Dr Sigmundus,' Beatrice replied, hoping desperately that once she began, the words of the ritual would come to her.

'And do you fully understand the purpose of this gift?'

'I do.'

'Then before all who are gathered here as witnesses, declare the Promises of Dr Sigmundus.'

Bea took a deep breath. 'Dr Sigmundus has promised us that where there was uncertainty, there shall be reassurance, where there was anxiety there shall be peace, where once we lived in fear of violence, in future we shall fear nothing...'

'Stop!' cried Miss Flambard angrily. 'The correct words are, "In future we shall fear no more", not we "shall fear nothing".'

'I'm sorry.'

'Very well, please continue.'

'Where once we lived in fear of violence, in future we shall fear no more...' Beatrice paused as her memory of the words withered away. Miss Flambard raised one eyebrow. 'Where once we lived in fear of violence, in future we shall fear no more,' Beatrice repeated. 'Where once the nations of the world...'

'Oh for heaven's sake, Beatrice, the part about the nations of the world comes much later. You haven't learned this at all, have you?'

'I tried, miss.'

'Well you didn't try hard enough. I'm afraid you've let yourself down badly this afternoon, Beatrice, and not just yourself. I know this is only a rehearsal but it's still a very important occasion and you have lowered the tone for all of us. Please go and sit at the back and listen carefully to the others.'

Bea felt herself flushing bright red as she went and sat down.

Francesca was next in line and, of course, her recital of the Promises was word perfect. When she had finished, Miss Flambard stepped forward, holding a sweet in one hand and a tumbler of water in the other. Francesca solemnly took the sweet, placed it in her mouth, bowed to Miss Flambard then, smiling smugly to herself, took a seat in the front row in respectful silence. One by one, the remaining students repeated the performance, most of them flawlessly.

By the end, Miss Flambard had recovered her good

humour. 'Well done,' she told them. 'There will be another rehearsal next week and this time I hope there will be no hitches.' Her eyes sought out Bea as she said this.

On the way home Bea thought about the secret Miss Flambard had revealed to them – the fact that the reliquary contained some of Dr Sigmundus's hair. She remembered the way the class had reacted and she shook her head in disbelief.

'Why can't I feel like that?' she asked herself.

When she got back, her mother was sitting at the kitchen table drinking a cup of tea.

'What are you doing back so early?' Bea asked, as she took off her coat and hung it over the back of a chair.

'I came home early because I've got something very serious to talk to you about,' her mother said. 'Sit down, please.'

Bea pulled out a chair and sat down opposite her mother. 'What's the matter?' she asked.

It turned out that it was Francesca's mother who had broken the news, coming up to Bea's mother with her features carefully arranged in a look of grave concern, insisting that she didn't want to worry her good friend but something had happened the previous night that could not be ignored, something to do with Beatrice.

Bea's mother had listened anxiously as Magdalena Belmonti had described how, after returning home from school, her daughter Francesca had come out with something very odd about Beatrice and a kitchen boy. Of course Magdalena had scolded her severely for making up such a wicked story but Francesca had been adamant that she wasn't making it up – it was all true. She had insisted that everyone at school was convinced Beatrice was involved in some sort of relationship with him. Well, naturally, Magdalena didn't believe a word of it herself – she knew what children were like, they made up all sorts of stories and convinced themselves they were true – but she realised that it was her duty to pass this news on to her good friend immediately because of the damage that was being done to poor Bea's reputation.

Bea could just picture how her mother must have looked as she listened to this: rigid with shame but trying desperately to give the impression that everything was under control, that there had just been some unfortunate misunderstanding.

'Well, Bea?' her mother said anxiously. 'Is there any truth in it?'

Bea sighed. There was no point in denying it. Too many people had seen Dante come up to her at the school gates. All she could do was try to emphasise the fact that he had approached her. She'd just been on her way to school, minding her own business, when this boy had walked up to her and started talking.

'But why did he pick on you?' Bea's mother demanded.

Bea shrugged. 'I don't know how other people's minds work,' she said.

'Well, what did he say to you?'

'I wasn't really listening.'

'You must have heard something.'

'He was just talking about his life.'

'You've never seen him before but he suddenly comes up to you and starts telling you about his life?'

'Well I have seen him once or twice before, actually, but only in the distance.'

'So you're telling me that there's absolutely nothing going on between you?'

'Of course there isn't.'

Her mother looked dissatisfied. 'Do you understand the damage this is doing to your reputation?' she said.

'I can't help it if some boy comes up and starts talking to me. I didn't ask him to.'

Her mother shook her head. 'The last thing this family needs is another scandal,' she muttered.

Bea frowned. 'What do you mean?' she asked.

'Just what I said. We don't need any scandals in this house,' her mother replied.

'No, you said the last thing this family needs is *another* scandal. So what else has happened?'

Bea's mother hesitated, and for the first time since they had sat down at the kitchen table, Bea felt the balance of power changing ever so slightly in her favour.

'Nothing,' her mother said at last. 'Nothing else has happened. All right then, if you say it was all a misunderstanding then I'll accept that, but if this boy approaches you again you're to have nothing to do with him. Is that clear?'

'Yes, Mum.'

'Just try to make us proud of you for—' She stopped,

but Bea knew that her mother had been about to say: just try to make us proud of you for once. 'Just think about the family,' she said, instead. Then she turned and left the kitchen without another word.

Bea breathed a sigh of relief and sat there for a long time thinking over what had just happened. Her mother had seemed rattled towards the end, there was no doubt about that, and it wasn't just because of what Francesca's mother had told her. Obviously, that was the direct cause of her anxiety, but there was something else too, something below the surface. Bea was sure that her mother really had said 'another scandal', even though she'd denied it. So what was all that about?

She went up to her room and lay on the bed, continuing to think about her mother's behaviour until, after a little while, she heard her father come home. Shortly afterwards her mother called her down for dinner. Without much enthusiasm, Bea went to join them in the dining room. Nobody spoke much. Her mother jumped every time Bea scraped her knife or fork against her plate, whereas her father had a distant look on his face. Bea began to hope that he had more important things on his mind and that he was not going to talk to her about the business with Dante at all. But after they'd finished eating, just as she was about to disappear upstairs again, her father seemed to come out of his trance.

'Bea, can I have a word with you?' he said.

'OK,' she replied cautiously.

'Let's go into the living room.'

He got up and led the way. Bea followed reluctantly while her mother carried the dishes out to the kitchen.

'Your mother told me about this business with the kitchen boy,' he began when they were sitting down.

Bea nodded, waiting for him to deliver his lecture.

'I don't want to tell you off about it,' he told her.

She frowned. What did he want to do then?

'People make mistakes,' her father continued. 'Nobody's perfect. The important thing is that you learn from your mistakes. Otherwise you end up repeating them. A mistake becomes a habit, a habit becomes a condition.'

Bea sighed. Why did he have to make everything sound like a medical matter?

'What I'm trying to tell you is that I don't blame you for what happened,' her father went on. 'When I was younger...' He hesitated. 'Well, let's say that I wasn't always as careful as I should have been about whom I associated with.'

Bea sat up. 'What do you mean?' she asked.

Her father looked as if he found this conversation difficult, but he carried on nonetheless. 'You'll probably get told this by somebody else one day,' he continued, 'so you might as well hear it from me first.'

'Get told what?' Now she was really interested.

Her father sighed. 'I don't know whether it's ever occurred to you, but I'm over-qualified for the post of junior doctor.'

Bea shook her head.

'No, I don't suppose it has. Why should it? I suppose

I like to think that people notice it about me but of course there's no reason why they should.'

'Notice what, Dad?'

'That I'm cleverer than the other junior doctors.' He shrugged. 'I'm not trying to boast,' he went on. 'Under the circumstances that's the last thing I should be doing. It's just a fact, that's all. I ought really to be a senior doctor by now. In fact, I should have been promoted years ago.'

'Then why haven't you been?'

'Scandal.'

Bea looked at him in amazement. She couldn't imagine anyone less likely to be involved in scandal than her father.

'What sort of scandal?' she asked.

'Not long after your mother and I were engaged, I became friends with one of the cleaners.'

Bea felt herself growing hot with embarrassment. What was her father trying to tell her?

'Oh, there wasn't anything to it, nothing emotional, I mean. Nothing like that at all. She was just an unusual young woman, too clever for her own good. She wanted to know all sorts of things that no one had taught her and she thought, because I'd been to university, I could help her understand the world. And I suppose I found that flattering. I got sucked in, you see, and started seeing her regularly. All we ever did was talk. I used to lend her books and we'd discuss them. Well, you know what Tarnagar is like. It wasn't long before somebody saw us and soon everyone knew. Your mother's family were very angry. I thought at first they were going to call off the engagement. But your mother stood by me and she talked them round. She was wonderful.'

'But what about the woman – the cleaner? What was her name?'

The ghost of a smile flickered across her father's face. 'Krystyna. Obviously we stopped seeing each other.'

'What happened to her?'

Her father shrugged. 'She still works in the library.'

'As a cleaner?'

'Yes.'

'So you must see each other sometimes.'

'Well, only very occasionally, but we take no notice of each other.'

Bea looked at him aghast, as the sadness of his story gradually sunk in – the little window that had opened in this unknown woman's life, only to be forcibly closed again just as the wind of change was beginning to enter.

'The reason I'm telling you this,' her father continued, 'is that I want you to see how damaging this sort of thing can be. I made a mistake and I've paid for it. Fortunately, my career wasn't completely ruined; your mother made sure of that. If she hadn't supported me, goodness knows where I'd be now. I might even be working as an orderly. You see, you get a reputation and people think you can't be trusted. That's why you have to make sure that you don't see this kitchen boy again. Do you understand?'

Bea nodded.

'It's very important, Bea.'

'I understand.'

'Good. I know we can rely on you.'

Bea went back upstairs, lay down on her bed and tried to sort out the questions that were filling her head. Had her father told her the whole truth? Had there really been nothing between him and this Krystyna woman except the desire for knowledge? And was that why Bea was so different from her classmates? Because she took after him?

Her father had learned from his mistake. He had made up his mind to fit in and, with her mother's help, he had succeeded. Was that what would happen to her? Would she, too, learn to fit in? And if she did so, would it make her happy?

Keeble was perched on his stool at the head of Corridor Y when Dante arrived with the afternoon meal. He had taken off one boot and was shaking it vigorously.

'Got a stone in my shoe,' he said, apologetically. 'Don't know where it came from. Have to do a lot of walking in this job.' He put the boot back on and laced it up tightly. Satisfied, he stood up with a grunt. 'You don't know how lucky you are working in the kitchen,' he went on. 'There's plenty of variety in a job like yours. You want to try being a security guard for a week, see how you'd like that.'

Dante said nothing. The idea that he was fortunate to be a kitchen boy was too ridiculous for words, but Keeble was given to bouts of self-pity and he was obviously going through one of them today.

Still grumbling to himself, Keeble led the way along the corridor and opened the cells of Salvador, Pavel and the Snake Charmer in turn, allowing Dante inside to bring them their food. Salvador was, as always, delighted with his meal. Pavel was asleep and snoring heavily. The Snake Charmer was having a bad day. She crouched on the bed, hugging her knees and staring wildly at the opposite corner of the room. She gave no sign whatsoever of having noticed Dante.

When all three meals had been delivered Dante expected Keeble to lead him back down the corridor, but instead he hesitated as if weighing up a suggestion.

Finally, he turned to Dante. 'Not allowed to feed the other one, are you?'

Dante shook his head.

'Too dangerous I expect. I still have to guard him, though. Doesn't matter if anything happens to me, does it? I'm only a security guard.'

Dante nodded. He couldn't think of anything to say in reply. But Keeble didn't really need a response. So long as he had someone to moan at, he was content.

'Do you want to take a look at him?' he went on.

Dante had not expected this. 'Through the spyhole, you mean?'

'Yeah. Can't do any harm just to have a look. Come on then'. He led the way to Ezekiel's cell and motioned towards the spyhole in the centre of the door. 'Help yourself.'

Dante slid back the cover and leaned forward to peer inside but what he saw made him jump back in dismay.

'What's the matter?' Keeble asked.

'He was standing on the other side of the door looking back at me,' Dante said. 'It was as if he knew I was going to look through the spyhole at that very moment and he was waiting for me.'

Keeble nodded. 'That's what he's like. Gives me the creeps.' He stepped forward, lifted the cover of the spyhole and put his eye to the glass.

'What's he doing now?' Dante asked.

'Sitting down in the furthest corner of the room,' Keeble said. He sounded disappointed.

'I don't understand how he knew I was going to look through the spyhole at that exact moment,' Dante said.

Keeble shrugged. 'Maybe he didn't. Maybe it was just coincidence. All the same,' he added as he led the way back along the corridor, 'I'm glad I'm on this side of the door. By rights, I ought to have someone else with me. When a patient's this dangerous you never can tell what he might do.'

They had reached the head of the stairs now. With a certain amount of fuss, Keeble lowered himself once more onto his stool while Dante carried on down the steps towards the kitchen. Only when he was completely out of sight did he allow himself to think about what had really happened. What he had told Keeble was true, but there was more to the episode. When he had lifted the cover of the spyhole and peered through the glass, Ezekiel Semiramis had been standing on the other side of the door, as if he had known perfectly well the moment when Dante would lift the cover of the spyglass and peer through, and with deliberately exaggerated movements of his lips, he had mouthed the word 'soon'. What did he mean by it? Was it just the raving of a madman? In his heart, that was not what Dante believed.

His mind turned immediately to Bea. He wondered what she was doing right then. Most likely she was on her way to school. What did she do there all day? he wondered. Reading and writing and number work, of course – but that was just for very young children. He knew that much. Perhaps she would be getting ready for her coming-of-age ceremony in a few weeks time. The thought of that filled Dante with sadness. Once she started taking Ichor all that rebelliousness would be washed away. She would learn to accept things as they were and she would want nothing more to do with him.

At that moment, Bea was standing outside the entrance to the Medical Library waiting for the cleaner to finish her shift. Like most public buildings on Tarnagar, the Medical Library was squat and ugly, built of unpainted concrete blocks with narrow windows through which it was just possible to glimpse row upon row of tall bookshelves. Between the bookcases were long tables at which many of the more ambitious junior doctors had already established themselves, even though the building had only opened to the public a matter of minutes ago.

Bea had left the house immediately after breakfast instead of waiting until the last possible minute, as was her habit. Her mother had been pleased at this apparent enthusiasm, taking it as a sign that her daughter was turning over a new leaf and trying to make up for the bad impression she had created at school. But instead of heading towards school, Bea had set off in the direction of Leader's Square.

Leader's Square was where many of the island's recreational facilities were situated. This was where a parade was held once a year on the birthday of Dr Sigmundus. Everyone took part: administrators, consultants, doctors, cleaners, security staff, kitchen workers – they all marched past the giant picture of the doctor and saluted. After the parade, adults dressed up as clowns organised competitions for the children.

When she was little, Bea had looked forward to those celebrations and had tried her hardest to be one of the fortunate children who came first, second or third in the races and received a winner's certificate with a picture of a smiling Dr Sigmundus. But as she got older she began to see it for what it was – an artificial occasion full of manufactured joy. Her enthusiasm faded; she no longer enjoyed the music of the junior doctors' brass band and choir and she stopped trying to win the competitions.

On one side of Leader's Square were the swimming baths and gymnasium. Exercise was taken seriously on Tarnagar and the gymnasium was one of the largest buildings on the island. Directly opposite stood the community centre where Bea's mother, along with most of her friends, attended flower-arranging classes twice a week and where her father sang in the junior doctors' choir on Friday nights. The Public Records Office, which held detailed files on every inhabitant of the island, occupied a third side of the square, and directly facing it was the Medical Library, outside which Bea now stood, waiting for the cleaner to leave the building.

She was not going to talk to the woman. She had

already made up her mind about that. She just wanted to see her, to know what she looked like. After she had recognised in the story of her father's brief rebellion the seeds of her own dissatisfaction, she simply had to find out more.

Just then a middle-aged woman dressed in the brown overalls of a cleaner came out of the front door of the library. She was thin and tired-looking with dark hair pulled back severely from her forehead, and shadows under her eyes. Bea had imagined that the woman who had tempted her father so greatly would be someone more glamorous. But perhaps this wasn't the right woman after all?

The woman walked away briskly and, hesitantly at first, then more determinedly, Bea began to follow her. She was conscious that time was limited. Very shortly she would have to turn and go back, or risk getting into more trouble at school. Suddenly, she made up her mind and caught up with the woman.

'Excuse me,' she said, 'I'm looking for Krystyna who used to clean the library,'

The woman stopped and looked at her suspiciously. 'What do you want with her?' she demanded.

'I just want to talk to her,' Bea said. 'If you could tell me where I might find her.'

'I am Krystyna,' the woman replied.

Bea hesitated. What did she want to say to this woman? It wasn't easy to put it into words. 'I think you used to know my father,' she said at last. 'His name is David Argenti.'

Krystyna's eyes widened with surprise. She nodded. 'You are quite correct. I used to know your father, but we have not spoken for a long time, years and years. Did he send you to speak to me?'

Bea shook her head. 'No. It was my idea. He told me about what happened and I...' she paused. 'I don't know why but I wanted to speak to you. I think I wanted to hear your side of the story, to know how you felt about it.'

'How I felt about it?' Krystyna smiled wryly. 'Well that's a first. But I'm afraid I have to go back to my flat now. I have another job delivering laundry which starts in half an hour. There's just time for a cup of tea in between.' Bea must have looked very disappointed because she added, 'You can come with me, if you like.'

Bea glanced at her watch. If she didn't leave right now, she would be late for school. Then she would have to think of some excuse. Krystyna looked at her, waiting for a decision.

Finally, Bea nodded, 'Thank you,' she said.

Krystyna's flat was in one of a series of identical apartment blocks which had been built for cleaners and other domestic staff. The walls had once been painted pale pink and blue, like some gigantic birthday cake, but the paint had long begun to flake. Now the block looked hopelessly shabby and rundown. Several of the letters on the front which once read 'Tranquil Mansions' had fallen off, and the little square of grass at the front was overgrown.

Bea followed Krystyna through the front door, past

a handwritten 'Out Of Order' sign taped to the front of the lift and up the stairs to the sixth floor. Krystyna opened the door of a tiny, stuffy little apartment and led the way into a kitchen scarcely big enough for them both to stand up in. The sink was full of dirty dishes.

Krystyna looked embarrassed. 'My daughter,' she said apologetically. 'She's never been very tidy.' She picked up a kettle, filled it with water and set it to boil. Then she began washing the cups and plates in the sink. 'So what is it you want me to tell you?' she asked.

'Your side of the story,' Bea said.

Krystyna smiled ruefully. 'There's not much to tell. It was before you were born. Your father was one of the first into the library every morning and one day I got talking to him. I don't recall exactly how it started. I was on my way out and he was on his way in and I think he must have said something about the cold. Yes, I remember now. He spoke about the heating in the library. It wasn't working properly and I made some sort of reply. That was all. But over the next few weeks we regularly exchanged a few words and soon we were having longer conversations.'

She put out two mugs for tea, without asking whether Bea wanted any.

'He spoke to me as if I were a human being,' she went on. 'That was what I noticed right away. The others either just ignored me completely or treated me as if I was a lower form of life. But your father, he was polite and kind.'

She poured boiling water into the mugs and added some milk, then waited for the tea to gain colour before taking out the tea bag and dropping it in the bin. She handed one of the mugs to Bea.

'Let's go into the living room. There's more space in there.'

There was more space, but most of it was taken up with an old brown sofa and an armchair. Krystyna sat down in the chair and gestured to Bea to sit on the sofa.

'I don't want to give the wrong impression,' she continued. 'There was never anything physical between your father and me. It was all up here.' She tapped her forehead with her finger. 'I was surrounded by books. I could see them, pick them up and dust them, but I could never take them out and read them. I told your father that once, and he asked me whether I really wanted to read them. So I said yes, of course. Not so much the medical textbooks but the books in the general section, the ones that dealt with history and philosophy. So he took them out and lent them to me. Of course most of them had been heavily censored and they only dealt with news or ideas that had been approved by the government, but I didn't know that then. I thought the library held the key to all the knowledge in the world and I wanted that knowledge.'

'My father said you used to talk about books together,' Bea went on.

Krystyna nodded. 'Oh yes, we talked and talked. Mostly it was me asking him questions and him answering them. There was so much I didn't know, and I thought that if I could discover some of that missing information, I could change my life here on Tarnagar. I know that sounds stupid but I was only young. I hadn't learned what life is really like.'

'How did you get found out?'

'People saw us. Tongues began to wag. One day he didn't come to the library. Instead, I got a summons to see the cleaning supervisor. She said it had come to her attention that I'd been abusing the library facilities – those were the words she used – by taking out books intended for the medical staff. My wages were reduced and it was made clear that if it happened again I would lose my job completely. After that I didn't see your father again for months. Then I saw him at the Birthday Parade on Leader's Day. He saw me, too, but he looked the other way.' She sighed.

'I'm sorry,' Bea said.

'Why are you sorry? It wasn't your fault. You weren't even born. Besides, I don't blame your father. What else could he do? I am sure his career must have suffered, just as mine did. No doubt he was told what would happen if there was any repeat of the incident. No, he made the wisest choice. And I expect he'd be very unhappy if he knew that you had come looking for me, wouldn't he?'

'Yes.'

'So you'd better go now.'

Bea nodded and stood up.

Krystyna stood up, too. For a moment the two of them

stood there face to face. There were tears in Krystyna's eyes. She put out her hand and touched Bea very lightly on the cheek.

'You look just like him,' she said.

A CONSPIRACY

When Dante walked into the kitchen after taking the slops to the pigs, there was an air of celebration about the place. People were standing around with smiles on their faces, their work abandoned. They were chatting and making jokes as if a holiday had been declared. It turned out that Nathaniel had announced his engagement to Polly. Mr Cuddy, in an uncharacteristic burst of generosity, had sent Jerome down to the cellar for a bottle of wine so they could all drink a toast to the happy couple.

'One of the bottles from the front, mind,' Mr Cuddy had added. 'Don't touch any of the vintage stuff. That's strictly for the senior administrators.'

Jerome had taken the keys and disappeared for a long time, finally coming back with a cobwebbed bottle, which Mr Cuddy scrutinised carefully before opening. Then he brought out the glasses that were used on Leader's Day, very carefully poured a little wine into five of them and handed them round: Nathaniel first, since the celebration was in his honour, then himself, followed by Marsyas, Jerome and Ivan.

'What about Dante?' Nathaniel asked good-naturedly. 'We can't leave him out.'

Mr Cuddy grimaced, picked up another wine glass, filled it with tap water and handed it to Dante.

'Now then everybody,' he said, 'I would like to propose a toast to Nathaniel and his bride-to-be. You all know I've had my disagreements with Polly in the past and you've probably heard me speak some harsh words about her from time to time. But she's a capable girl, as anyone can see, and a hard worker when she wants to be. I've no doubt she'll make a very good wife for our Nathaniel. So let's all raise our glasses and drink to their health: Nathaniel and Polly.'

'When's the big day?' Marsyas asked when the toast had been drunk.

'We haven't decided yet,' Nathaniel told him. 'Some time in August, I think.'

'Did you get down on one knee to pop the question?' Ivan asked.

'Don't you believe it,' Jerome replied before Nathaniel could open his mouth. 'She probably asked him.'

Nathaniel looked indignant. 'She never did!' he insisted angrily.

'Now then, that's enough,' Mr Cuddy said. He finished his wine and put the glass down on the table. 'Time we got back to work.'

The others drank up and reluctantly returned to the business of preparing and cooking food. Mr Cuddy held the wine bottle up to the light and, satisfied that there was enough left to be worth bothering with, he pushed the cork back into the neck, put the bottle under his arm and disappeared through the door.

'No prizes for guessing where he's off to,' said Ivan.

The others nodded. Mr Cuddy would no doubt lock the door of his office to all comers for the next half-hour. Dante decided to seize the opportunity for a break of his own. He picked up a bucket of vegetable peelings and carried them outside. As soon as he was out of sight, he put the bin down and made his way to the woods.

It didn't bother him that Mr Cuddy had only given him water when everybody else had had wine. So why did he feel as though he had a lump in his throat? He ought to feel pleased for Nathaniel – he did feel pleased for him; but at the same time a powerful sense of loneliness was overwhelming him. He found himself remembering what Polly had said, that she reckoned she could trust him because he wasn't important enough to make trouble for anyone. And it struck him that he would probably never get married – not that he wanted to anyway – but even if he did, who else was as low down the hierarchy as he was?

Thinking these dark thoughts, he found he'd made his way, without even realising it, to the huge, misshapen willow tree where he'd first met Bea. He bent down, put his hand into the hole in the trunk and rummaged around among the leaves. To his surprise he felt something there. He pulled it out and held it up. It was a handkerchief exactly like the one she had given him. There was even the same little piece of embroidery in the corner. She wanted to see him. A sense of delight stole over Dante and a huge grin spread across his face. He stuffed the handkerchief in his pocket, turned round

108

and walked back to the kitchen. They could treat him how they liked now; it didn't matter. He had something to look forward to.

If Bea had known the effect her handkerchief had had on Dante, she might have felt a little less gloomy as she sat in her bedroom, trying to decide when she had begun to question everything around her. She remembered one Leader's Day celebration years ago. She had been walking with her parents, holding their hands as they came in sight of an enormous banner of Dr Sigmundus above the entrance to the athletics track. Bea had turned to her father and asked him why the picture of Dr Sigmundus never changed from one year to the next.

'Doesn't he get any older?' she'd said.

She must have been about eight or nine at the time and she could clearly recall how, for the briefest of moments, her father's mouth had curved upwards in a smile. Had he been proud of her?

But her mother had answered for him. 'Dr Sigmundus is a very remarkable man,' she had told Bea. 'He has achieved mental equilibrium.'

'What does that mean?'

'It means that he has a completely healthy mind and, as we all know, a healthy mind and a healthy body go together.'

'And that's why he doesn't get older?'

'Of course he gets older, Bea, but he doesn't show it

like other people do, because there is no conflict in his mind.'

'What's conflict?'

'Conflict is when you want something that you can't have.'

'Like when I want sweets but you say I can't have them.'

'Exactly.'

Bea had not really understood what her mother meant. She had got the impression that Dr Sigmundus's unchanged features were a result of his not eating sweets and later, when her parents had bought her some candyfloss as a treat, Bea had shaken her head, determined to follow her Leader's example.

Now she wondered how old Dr Sigmundus really was. You couldn't tell from the history books. They were deliberately vague. The picture that dominated every public space on Tarnagar showed a man in the prime of his life, handsome, athletic, with an expression that was somehow both stern and kind. But perhaps he didn't look like that at all? How could anyone who hadn't seen him in person possibly know?

Had her father also been plagued by thoughts like this when he was her age? Was that why he had risked public scandal? If so, he had long ago buried his doubts in a part of his mind so secret even he no longer had access to it.

She had tried to find out more about the episode, but he refused to go into any further detail, only repeating what he'd already said. When she had asked him if he didn't sometimes think Tarnagar was a horrible place and wish he could live somewhere entirely different, he had grown angry, shouting at her that she wasn't listening, that the society she lived in was the most advanced in the history of mankind and that their work on Tarnagar was of the utmost importance.

'What we are doing on this island is standing guard over the mental health of our people! It's a very grave responsibility and we are honoured to have been entrusted with it. That's what you need to understand.'

There was a knock on her door and her mother stepped into the room.

'I'm going out to my flower-arranging class in a minute, Bea,' she said.

Bea had been counting on just that.

'And your father has already left for his choir practice. So you'll be on your own this evening.'

'I'm on my own every Wednesday evening,' Bea pointed out.

'Of course you are. It's just that... Well I was wondering if you didn't spend too much time by yourself.'

'I like being by myself.'

Her mother frowned. 'I'm not sure that's healthy,' she said.

That word – healthy – Bea was so tired of hearing it.

'I've got plenty of homework to do,' she replied.

'Yes, but it is possible to study too hard, you know. Why don't you come with me?'

'Oh Mum! I don't want to go to flower-arranging.'

'Well you needn't say it like that,' her mother objected. 'Quite a few girls go with their mothers, especially if they're getting close to their coming-of-age ceremonies. They want to be involved in all the arrangements, that's only natural, and the flowers are a very important part of the celebration.'

'I'm sure you'll do a very good job on my behalf,' Bea said.

Her mother sighed. 'Well, don't say I don't take you anywhere,' she said. She turned and went back downstairs.

A few minutes later Bea heard the sound of the front door closing. She made herself wait ten minutes, so that she could be absolutely sure her mother was nowhere in sight. Then she put on her coat and left the house.

Earlier that day she had decided to tell Dante about her visit to the Medical Library and she had slipped into the woods after school to leave the handkerchief. While she was on her way home, an idea had come to her that was so shocking, she had stopped in her tracks and gasped. It was the most dangerous thing she had ever imagined. Yet, the more she thought about it, the more it fascinated her. She longed to know what Dante would think of it. But would he have visited the tree that afternoon?

She needn't have worried. He was waiting for her when she got there.

'How long have you been here?' she asked.

He shrugged. 'About half an hour.'

'Sorry. I had to wait for my parents to go out.'

112

'It doesn't matter.' He looked at her expectantly.

'Something happened that I wanted to tell you about,' she explained.

'What was it?'

Bea hesitated. 'You promise to keep it secret?' she said.

'Of course.'

'Say it,' Bea insisted. 'Say, "I promise to keep what you tell me a secret."'

'I promise to keep what you tell me a secret.'

Satisfied, Bea described what her father had told her about his friendship with a cleaner and how she had waited outside the Medical Library and had spoken to her. Dante listened without comment.

'You don't seem very surprised,' she said when she had finished.

'I've already heard something similar,' he explained.

Bea looked a little deflated. 'What did you hear?' she demanded.

'A girl who works in the laundry – Polly, her name is – she told me that her mother was friends with one of the doctors when she was younger, and that he used to borrow books for her.'

'What did you think when you heard it?'

Dante shrugged. 'I was surprised, I suppose.'

'That's all? Just surprised?'

'Yes. Why? What else should I have felt?'

Bea shook her head. 'I don't know. Maybe it's different for you.'

'What did you feel then?' Dante asked.

113

'I felt shocked but reassured at the same time because it proves that there's a reason for all these thoughts that keep popping into my head; they don't just come from nowhere. It's in my blood. And it also proves that this whole business of certain families being doctors and certain families being cleaners with nothing ever changing is all just completely artificial.'

'Yes,' Dante agreed. 'That's what I thought.'

'And yet all my life I've been brought up to think that whatever else you do, you shouldn't mix with those who are beneath you.'

'You mixed with me,' Dante pointed out. 'I'm as far beneath you as it's possible to get.'

'That just happened by accident. Besides, you've no idea how much trouble I've got into at school because of it.'

'I didn't mean to cause problems for you,' Dante said, stiffly.

'I'm not complaining. I'm just thinking out loud. The woman I spoke to, Krystyna, she was a perfectly intelligent person, and in many ways I think she understood me better than my own mother but she's only ever going to be a cleaner. Once upon a time she believed things might be different and that belief was like a flower opening in her life. But then someone stepped on the flower and crushed it and now she just accepts things as they are because there's nothing else she can do.'

Dante nodded. 'That's what it's like on Tarnagar,' he said. 'Nothing's ever going to change.'

'Unless we make it change,' Bea told him.

Dante looked sceptical. 'How could we possibly do that?' he asked.

'I've had an idea,' Bea said.

'What is it?'

'I've thought of a way you could talk to Ezekiel Semiramis without anyone knowing, but it's extremely dangerous.'

Dante's eyes widened with interest. 'Tell me anyway,' he told her, eagerly. 'I'm prepared to take the risk, whatever it is.'

Bea shook her head. 'You don't understand,' she replied. 'I'm the one who's going to be in danger.'

THE RECOVERY ROOM

The following morning, as Bea walked from her classroom to the playing fields, she felt as if her real self, which had been locked inside her for so long, was refusing to lie low any longer. The plan she had come up with the previous day both terrified and thrilled her and for the first time in days, she allowed herself a secret smile. At worst she would be spared the ordeal of running up and down the hockey pitch pointlessly for the next hour, knowing that no one would pass the ball to her, but trying to pretend she was still taking part in the game. At best, she might find out something about the ruined city that had haunted her dreams for so long.

But first she would have to convince her games mistress. Miss Galahad was so enthusiastic about running around in the open air, she found it difficult to believe that other people might not enjoy it quite as much as she did. Bea would have to get the tone of her voice and the expression on her face exactly right.

She hung about in the changing room, taking a long time with buttons and laces until all the other girls were on their way out of the pavilion. Then, with a suitably hangdog expression on her face, she approached Miss Galahad.

'Please, miss,' she declared in her most feeble voice, 'I don't feel very well.'

In her short hockey skirt, singlet, and woolly socks, Miss Galahad presented a formidable figure. Even in middle age, she was a powerfully built woman and the muscles on her calves bulged from years spent driving reluctant girls up and down the playing fields. She towered over Bea, looking down on her as if she were some lower form of life.

'What exactly is wrong with you, Beatrice?' she demanded, sternly.

'I've got a terrible headache.'

'You look all right to me. I should think a bit of exercise might do you good.'

'But I feel like I'm going to be sick,' Bea went on. 'Honestly, miss, I really am ill.'

'Oh very well,' Miss Galahad said, impatiently. 'You'd better stay in the pavilion. Have you got some homework you can be getting on with?'

'Yes, miss.'

'All right then.'

She turned and went outside, breaking into a jog as soon as she was out of the door and blowing furiously on the silver whistle that she always wore on a string round her neck. Bea watched from the doorway until she was quite certain Miss Galahad's entire attention was occupied by organising the girls into two teams of players, then she made her way to the shower room at the back of the pavilion, opened the window and carefully climbed out.

The pavilion backed onto an overgrown privet hedge and on the other side of that hedge was the bottom of Bea's garden. She found a spot where the hedge was at its thinnest, and, with some difficulty, forced her way through.

She crept along the length of the garden, keeping near the fence on the left-hand side where she hoped she was out of sight of the upstairs windows. Just as she had expected, the back door of her house was unlocked. She opened it with as little noise as possible and stepped inside. Her father would be upstairs in his office at this very minute going through the endless columns of statistics he was required to present to his superiors at regular intervals. He would be completely absorbed in his work. After lunch, as he had told her mother at the breakfast table, he would set off for the Old Clinic to assist in the Recovery Room, where patients were brought after receiving shock treatment. Bea had to get his keys and make her way there first. Dante would be waiting in the corridor outside and she would be able to let him inside. It would be up to him to find some sort of hiding place where he could remain unseen until Ezekiel Semiramis was wheeled in.

The doctors, her father among them, would carry out a variety of checks before leaving their patient secured to the bed. Once they were gone Dante could come out and ask all the questions he wanted to. Whether or not Ezekiel Semiramis would be in any condition to answer them was another matter, but Dante had been optimistic when they'd discussed it. He seemed convinced that the man's powers of recovery were significantly greater than those of other people.

Once she was sure he was safely hidden inside the Recovery Room, Bea would have to get back home as quickly as possible, replace the keys and return to the pavilion before anyone noticed she was gone. It had all sounded perfectly feasible when she'd described it to Dante the night before. Now, as she tiptoed into the sitting room where her father kept his keys, she felt much less confident.

She carefully opened the left-hand drawer of the sideboard, where the keys were kept. But, she had just picked them up and put them in her pocket when she heard someone coming down the stairs. In a few seconds her father would walk into the room and find her! What was she going to say? Moving as quickly and as quietly as she could, she pushed the drawer back in, then got down on her hands and knees and crawled into the space between the sofa and the wall.

Her father did not come straight into the living room. Instead, she heard him walking along the hall and then rummaging in the kitchen. A few moments later he left the kitchen and, to her dismay, came into the living room. Bea's heart was thumping wildly. From where she was hidden it was impossible to see very much. What was he doing? Had he heard her moving about and come downstairs to investigate?

Suddenly he spoke. 'There they are!' he said.

He went over to the coffee table and moved within her field of vision. She watched as he picked up his glasses from the table. There was a very strong chance that he would see her now if he turned in the wrong direction. But, to her relief, he straightened up, walked out of the room and went back upstairs again.

Bea crawled out from her hiding place and looked at her watch. It was eleven thirty-three already. Creeping out of the room into the hall, she let herself out of the front door and took a deep breath. Between her own front door and the entrance to the clinic she would be entirely out in the open.

While Bea was setting out for the main building, Dante was waiting nervously in the corridor outside the Recovery Room. Unlike her, he had no idea what he was going to say if anyone challenged him. As a member of the kitchen staff he had absolutely no business hanging around the corridors of the clinic, and whenever he remembered Mr Appollyon's parting words, he shuddered.

Although Dante did not possess a watch, there were clocks everywhere in the asylum and Mr Cuddy had made sure that Dante was able to tell the time. According to the clock on the wall it was twenty-five to twelve. So where on earth was Bea?

Just then a man appeared at the end of the corridor. Panic-stricken, Dante turned and began to walk away quickly in the opposite direction but the man called out, 'Hey you! Wait a minute!'

For a moment Dante considered running away.

Instead, he waited while the man caught up with him. He was tall and thin with a shock of long, rather untidy white hair and there were three silver stripes on the breast pocket of his white coat, indicating that he was a senior doctor.

'What's your name?' he asked.

'Dante.'

'Position?'

'Kitchen boy.'

The doctor frowned. 'Kitchen boy? What on earth are you doing in the clinic?'

'I was looking for Mr Cuddy, sir, the catering manager. Somebody told me he was here.'

'The catering manager? What would the catering manager be doing in the clinic?'

'I don't know, sir. I must have made a mistake. I'm sorry to bother you.'

'This is a restricted area,' the doctor continued, 'especially at the moment. I shall have to escort you off the premises. Come along.'

With a sinking feeling, Dante fell into step beside the tall, white-haired figure.

Only seconds after they had disappeared around the corner, Bea arrived at the other end of the corridor. With no sign of Dante, she had no idea what to do next. Should she wait for him? And if so, for how long?

As she stood there nervously glancing up and down the corridor, she began to feel angry. She was the one who was putting herself at greatest risk. All he had to do was to turn up on time. And he couldn't even manage that! If she were caught standing outside the Recovery Room, she could imagine what her father would say. Yet that might be the least of her worries. Bea was sometimes frightened of her father, especially when he was in one of his tempers, but she knew that there were many more people that her father himself was frightened of.

She became conscious of a squeaking noise in the distance that seemed to be gradually getting louder. Suddenly she realised what it was: a trolley was being pushed along a corridor – doctors or orderlies were coming this way! She had only an instant to act. Without even thinking, she put her hand in her pocket, took out the key and let herself into the Recovery Room.

It was a big, mostly bare room with a number of empty beds against one wall. Beside the beds was an array of machinery for monitoring the patients' responses. Against the opposite wall were a series of steel cupboards. Had she trapped herself completely? What was she going to do if they opened the door and discovered her?

Hearing the voices getting closer, she ran across the room and opened one of the steel cupboards. Every inch was stacked with medical supplies. She tried the next one, with the same result. But the third cupboard was empty and there was just enough room for her on the bottom shelf. She scrambled inside and pulled the door shut behind her, leaving just the tiniest crack open for air. A moment later the door of the room opened.

Through the crack, she watched as two orderlies

pushed the trolley into the room. They were followed by a doctor and, to Bea's surprise, the director himself. A patient on the trolley was barely conscious. He had probably just received shock treatment. Was it Ezekiel Semiramis? Had he been taken for treatment earlier than her father had expected?

Bea watched as the orderlies undid the straps on the trolley, lifted the patient onto one of the beds, then fastened him in again. When they were sure he was thoroughly secured, the doctor began connecting him to the various machines designed to measure his heartbeat, pulse rate, temperature and other vital signs. It seemed to take an incredibly long time. Bea had pins and needles in one foot and she longed to stretch her legs. But the doctor took endless readings from the various dials and monitors beside the bed, writing them down laboriously on a chart.

At last he seemed satisfied and handed over the results to Mr Appollyon. The director studied them for some time. Then he dismissed the others.

After the doctor and the two orderlies had left the room, Mr Appollyon stood beside the patient for some time with his hands clasped in front of him. Bea wondered, desperately, how much longer her ordeal was going to last. Eventually he spoke.

'Well Mr Semiramis,' he began, 'Dr Zinoviev assures me that it is quite impossible for you to take in any information for at least another hour, but I'm not so sure. I think you are an extraordinary man, with extraordinary abilities, and I believe you may be perfectly able to understand what I have to say.' He leaned closer to the bed now and spoke in a low voice so that Bea could only just catch what he said. 'You have led us a merry dance for a long time. Now suddenly the dance has come to an end. What new game are you playing?'

He paused but the figure on the bed showed no sign of having heard him. He sighed. 'Sooner or later, you will tell us what you are up to,' he continued. 'You might as well make it easy on yourself by starting now. Think about it.' Then he straightened, turned, and walked briskly out of the room.

Bea waited for a little while in case he came back. When she was certain he was gone, she crawled out of her hiding place and made her way over to the bed. Ezekiel Semiramis was older than she had expected, and there was grey in his hair. He had a thin face, with hollow cheeks and a long, slightly hooked nose which reminded her a little of a bird of prey. He did not look well. His skin was an unhealthy grey colour, and there were beads of sweat on his forehead. Nevertheless, it was clear that they were taking no chances with him: straps secured him to the bed in half-a-dozen different places.

As she stood there looking down on him, his eyelids flickered open and two pale blue eyes gazed up at her with a look of surprising intensity.

'I'm sorry to disturb you, Mr Semiramis,' she said, 'but I need to talk to you. I'm a friend of Dante's.'

'You expect me to believe that?' He spoke in a hoarse

whisper, as if every word were an enormous effort.

'It's true. I promise you.'

Ezekiel Semiramis continued to regard her with the same suspicious look.

'I just want to know about the ruined city,' she told him.

The ghost of a smile played across his lips. 'Everybody wants to know about the ruined city,' he told her.

Bea felt a wave of frustration building up inside her. 'Look, I'm not like the others,' she said. 'I'm not trying to make you tell me something you don't want to. This isn't a trick.'

'Then what is it?'

'It's just that I keep dreaming that I'm standing in the middle of that city,' she said. She saw the look of surprise in his eyes but carried on. It was becoming easier to talk about dreaming now that she had broken the taboo. 'I used to think it was just a place I'd made up, somewhere that didn't really exist except in my head, until Dante told me what you said about his mother. Please, you have to tell me what it means.'

Now Ezekiel Semiramis was frowning as if he was not certain what to make of her. 'If what you say is true,' he told her, 'then it means there is a place in the ruined city for you. But that is very hard for me to believe; I came here to bring this news to Dante, not to you.'

Bea struggled to make sense of what he said, but it didn't seem to add up.

'You didn't come here,' she pointed out. 'You

were brought here. They captured you. This is the asylum, remember.'

The same wry smile flickered across his face. 'They could not have captured me unless I let them. That is what puzzles your director. Believe me, I came here of my own free will and I will leave in the same way. Perhaps I will walk out of here this very night. If that is what I choose, there is nothing they can do to stop me.'

Bea shook her head. 'I'm afraid it isn't that easy,' she said. 'They've decided you're a serious risk to the community. They'll never let you go.'

'They will have no choice,' Ezekiel replied.

Bea sighed. He was either completely crazy or still in a state of shock. Probably both. She looked at her watch.

'I'm going to have to go now,' she told him. 'I'm probably in terrible trouble already.'

He gave no sign of having heard her.

She crossed the room, opened the door a crack and peered out. There was no one in the corridor. So she stepped outside and closed the door behind her. Then she began to retrace the route she had taken a little earlier, walking as quickly as she could without drawing too much attention to herself. Even so, she knew that the other girls would have finished their game by now. They would be back in the pavilion, taking their showers.

First she had to sneak back into her house and replace the key. She dreaded encountering her father again but it was surprisingly easy. He was completely absorbed in his work. Afterwards, there seemed little point in struggling through the hedge and climbing back into the pavilion through the window. Her absence would already have been noticed. Better to brazen it out.

Miss Galahad was waiting when she walked through the pavilion door. She looked very cross indeed.

'Beatrice Argenti, where on earth have you been?' she demanded.

'I went home because I felt sick,' Bea said.

'And who gave you permission?'

'No one, miss.'

'You mean you just walked out of the pavilion without asking anyone?'

'Yes miss. I felt really terrible.'

'Well, you seem perfectly all right now.'

'I'm feeling a bit better.'

'What you don't seem to understand, young lady, is that you can't just go wandering off on your own whenever you feel like it.'

'I know miss, I'm sorry. I just—'

'Don't interrupt, Beatrice. You will copy out chapter one of the Promises of Dr Sigmundus and bring it to me first thing tomorrow morning. Along with a note from your parents testifying to the fact that you were with them for the last hour. Is that clear?'

'Yes, miss.'

'Good. Now you'd better make your way to your next lesson before you miss any more of your education.'

A DISTURBANCE IN THE NIGHT

That night Bea lay in bed feeling immensely sorry for herself. It had taken her over two hours to copy out the Promises of Dr Sigmundus and by the time she had finished, her hand was aching. But the ordeal of passing off a forged note from her father still awaited her the following morning.

As she lay there, worrying about what would happen if Miss Galahad decided to talk to her parents about the incident, there was a sharp tap against the window pane. A moment later it came again. Puzzled, she sat up and switched on the bedside lamp. According to the clock it was after midnight. She got out of bed and went to the window to investigate. When she drew back the curtains she could dimly see someone standing in the garden outside. It was Dante.

As quickly as she could, she switched off her light, put on her dressing gown and slippers, and crept downstairs. Several of the stairs creaked and she froze each time, waiting for her parents to appear but, to her relief, they remained sound asleep.

Dante was waiting at the back door. He opened his mouth to speak but she put her finger to her lips and led him through the garden towards the tool shed. It was a dark night with only a fragment of moon glinting in the sky like a sliver of bone, and the inside of the shed was almost pitch black. Dante swore softly as he scraped his shin against a box.

'Keep your voice down,' Bea told him.

'It's so dark in here.'

'Just as well. I don't want anyone to see us. I'm in enough trouble already, thanks to you. '

'I'm sorry,' Dante said. 'A senior doctor turned up while I was waiting for you and he made me leave. What did you do?'

She told him what had happened.

'You didn't find out anything about my mother?'

Bea felt a twinge of guilt. In her anxiety, she had forgotten all about Dante's mother.

'He didn't say anything that made any sense,' she replied evasively. 'If you ask me, he's completely crazy. He actually told me he'd come here especially to speak to you and he could leave any time he wanted to.'

But Dante was not prepared to give up hope so easily. 'If he's just another mentally ill patient, what was Mr Appollyon doing in that room?' Dante insisted.

'Ezekiel Semiramis knows something that Mr Appollyon wants to find out, that's obvious,' Bea told him. 'But he was talking complete nonsense when I spoke to him.'

'He'd just had shock treatment, remember. Most patients can't even talk at all.'

'I'm not denying he's an unusual man,' Bea conceded.

'I just don't think he's going to be any help to you or me.'

'Don't you want to find out about the ruined city?'

Bea shook her head. 'I shouldn't have told you about it,' she said.

'So you're just going to give up?'

'I just want to be like everybody else. I've decided I want to be happy.'

'You think everybody else is happy?'

'They fit in. Maybe if I started trying to do the same, things might be easier for me.'

Dante said nothing, but now that Bea's eyes had adjusted to the darkness, she could see the disappointment written across his face. She hated to think that she was the one who had put it there, but she had decided she wasn't brave enough to be different. It was too lonely. Tomorrow she would go back to school and find a way to make the others start talking to her again.

Dante sighed. 'Well thanks for trying,' he said. He opened the door of the shed and they both stepped outside. The moment they did so, bells began to ring furiously, shattering the silence of the night.

They stopped in their tracks. 'What's going on?' Bea asked.

'It's coming from the direction of the clinic,' Dante told her. 'Could it be the alarm bell? I've never heard it ring before.'

'What does it mean?'

'I think it means that a patient has escaped!'

'Ezekiel Semiramis! It has to be him.'

Dante nodded, excitedly. 'I'd better get back. There'll be security guards everywhere in no time.'

They parted without another word. Bea made her way back to the house as quickly as she could. Even so, she had only just let herself into the kitchen when her father appeared. He was fully dressed but he still looked half asleep.

'What are you doing up?' he demanded.

'I heard the alarm.'

Her mother appeared just then. She was still in her pyjamas. 'Bea, I want you to go back to bed right now,' she said. 'If there's a security alert, the last thing they need is children wandering around.' She sounded anxious.

'Has a patient escaped?'

'We don't know. Your father's going to find out. Now go on, back to bed.'

Bea went back up to her room and got into bed but she was determined to find out what had happened. Her father was gone for about half an hour and, despite her resolution, she was beginning to drift off to sleep when she heard the front door opening. Immediately, she roused herself and got out of bed. Her mother was at the top of the stairs.

'I thought you'd be asleep by now,' she said.

'I'm too nervous to sleep,' Bea told her. She followed her mother downstairs and they found her father in the kitchen, making a pot of tea.

'What's going on?' her mother asked.

'Ezekiel Semiramis has escaped,' her father said, bluntly.

Her mother looked shocked. 'How is that possible?'

Her father shook his head. 'No one can understand it. The guard was discovered locked in the cell. I heard it from Dr Zinoviev himself.'

'Was the guard injured?'

'He doesn't seem to have been. Do you want a cup of tea?'

Her mother shook her head impatiently. 'But what did he say when they questioned him?'

Her father poured himself a cup and added three spoonfuls of sugar, even though he normally only took one. 'That's the strange thing,' he said. 'The man can't remember anything.'

'What do you mean?'

'Just what I say. He doesn't know how he ended up locked in the cell.'

'It doesn't make any sense,' her mother said. She looked profoundly agitated, and Bea wondered whether she might not burst into tears at any moment. Her father, on the other hand, seemed to be moving in slow motion, as though he had been stunned. As he sipped his tea the sound of barking could be heard in the distance. Bea knew what that meant: the dogs had been set loose. She had seen those dogs. They were kept in kennels on the farm. There were six, savage-looking creatures.

'He won't get far,' her father said. 'They'll find him before morning.'

Her mother nodded. 'Of course they will,' she agreed.

Bea was not so sure. Ezekiel Semiramis had done exactly what he had promised. And now that he was free, she wondered what kind of havoc he would unleash on Tarnagar.

TORTURE

The next morning everyone at school was so busy talking about the shocking events of the night, they even managed to forget about the scandal of Bea and the kitchen boy. People didn't go so far as to actually speak to her but they did allow her to hang around on the edge of their group, listening to the gossip as it passed from person to person and became more lurid with each retelling. Some people said that the guard had been found hanged in the cell. Others maintained that his throat had been cut. One boy even insisted that the man's arms and legs had been cut off.

Bea let them believe what they wanted to. The one thing everyone did agree on was that it would not be long before Ezekiel Semiramis was back where he belonged. This sentiment was repeated over and over again, as people sought to reassure themselves that there was no real danger.

Despite this constant reassurance, an air of anxiety hung over the school. Even the teachers seemed ill at ease. Miss Galahad accepted Bea's forged note and her handwritten copy of the Promises of Dr Sigmundus without comment, whereas ordinarily she might have been expected to deliver another long lecture. Mr Samphire completely forgot to ask the class to hand in their essays. The complex machinery that kept Tarnagar working with such clinical efficiency had been disturbed by the unpredictable behaviour of one man and now everyone seemed temporarily to have lost confidence in what they were doing.

Bea enjoyed witnessing the state of nervous tension that seemed to have gripped the whole school, taking the spotlight off her for a while. The respite did not last very long, however. In the middle of the afternoon their maths lesson was interrupted by the appearance of Mrs Minniver, the headteacher.

Mr Scallion, their maths teacher, an edgy individual at the best of times, visibly jumped when the door opened and she stepped into the room.

'Sorry to interrupt you, Mr Scallion,' she said. 'I've just come to collect Beatrice Argenti. Beatrice, please follow me.'

Beatrice felt herself turn bright red and every head in the class swivelled round to stare as she stood up and walked to the front of the class. It was unheard of for the headteacher herself to come looking for a student. Clearly Bea was in serious trouble.

But Mrs Minniver was giving nothing away. 'Please carry on with your lesson,' she told them as she held the door open for Bea.

When they were out in the corridor, Bea spoke. 'Please, miss, I don't understand what's happening.'

'I'm not altogether sure I do, either, Beatrice,'

Mrs Minniver said, in a grave tone.

'Am I in trouble, miss?'

'I'm afraid you are, Bea, but we'll discuss the matter in my office, not out here in the corridor.'

When they reached the office, Mrs Minniver opened the door and stepped aside to let Bea enter first. To her horror, Bea saw that Mr Appollyon was sitting behind the desk. He looked up at her and gave an icy smile. Mrs Minniver stepped into the room behind Bea and closed the door. Then she sat down on a chair to one side.

'Sit down, Beatrice,' Mr Appollyon said.

Bea sat.

'I expect you know what this is all about.'

'No, sir.'

Mr Appollyon looked irritated. 'Why does everyone always waste my time?' he asked.

Bea said nothing. He obviously didn't know everything yet. That was why he was here: to find out more. Well, she had no intention of making it easy for him. He opened a file on the desk in front of him and took out a piece of paper which he unfolded and held out towards her. She saw that it was the note she had handed to Miss Galahad that morning.

'Recognise this little forgery?' he asked.

Bea opened her mouth to reply but he forestalled her. 'You needn't bother making up some elaborate story. I have already spoken to your parents. They know nothing about your absence yesterday. So perhaps you'd like to tell me what you really got up to when you disappeared yesterday.'

'I went for a walk because I had a headache.'

'Quite a long walk, it seems. You were seen in the area of the Recovery Room.'

'I didn't think about where I was going.'

'Really?'

'Yes, sir.'

Mr Appollyon shook his head. 'I believe you did think about where you were going, Beatrice. I believe you thought very carefully about it.'

'I just wandered about,' Bea insisted.

Mr Appollyon turned to the file again. This time what he took out made Bea gasp, despite her resolution not to give any information away. It was her drawing of the ruined city.

'Where did you get that from?' she demanded.

'I searched your room, of course.' He spoke as if he were talking to an infant.

'You had no right to do that!'

'That's where you're wrong, Beatrice. I have every right. Dr Sigmundus has given me complete and absolute authority on this island. There is no limit to my powers. Did no one ever tell you that? I may look wherever I please in the interests of security, including your bedroom. Now then, what exactly is this supposed to be?'

'It's a drawing.'

Only the twitch of a muscle on the left side of Mr Appollyon's face betrayed the fact that he was angered by her answer.

'I can see that,' he said, continuing in the same calm, measured voice. 'What I want to know is where you got the idea from.'

'From my dreams,' Bea said.

Mrs Minniver, who had been sitting in silence throughout Mr Appollyon's questions looked very uncomfortable when she heard this. She opened her mouth to protest but Mr Appollyon raised his right hand and she fell silent.

Slowly and very deliberately, Mr Appollyon tore the picture into pieces and dropped them into the bin.

'There will be no more images like this when you come of age,' he told her.

Bea thought of the hours she had spent working on that drawing and the pleasure it had given her when it was finished. She badly wanted to say something that would burst the bubble of Mr Appollyon's arrogance.

'Some people still have dreams after they receive Ichor,' she pointed out.

He smiled contemptuously. 'Everyone's dreams cease when they come of age.'

'Dante's didn't,' she snapped back. The words were out of her mouth before she realised what she had said. Too late, she saw a gleam come into Mr Appollyon's eyes.

'How very interesting!' he said. 'I think you'd better tell me everything that you and Dante have been up to.'

Bea bitterly regretted her outburst but it was too late to do anything about it now.

'We haven't been up to anything,' she told him. Even

to her own ears, it did not sound very convincing.

'Then how do you know he still has dreams?'

'I just made it up.'

Mr Appollyon raised one eyebrow. 'That's a very stupid thing to say.'

'I'm a stupid girl.'

'Ah, but I don't think you are, Beatrice. On the contrary, I think you're a very intelligent young woman. You know, I'm sure you'd rather all this unpleasantness was behind you, wouldn't you?'

He leaned more closely towards her, his voice taking on a smooth, coaxing tone, as if he were a favourite uncle come to offer her a birthday treat. 'Let's not drag it out any longer than is strictly necessary, shall we? As you can see, I already know a great deal about you. All you have to do is clear up one or two details for me. Then you can go back to your classroom and this whole unpleasant incident will be forgotten. Now, I believe you were trying to see Ezekiel Semiramis, weren't you?'

'Why would I want to do that?'

The calm surface of Mr Appollyon's behaviour suddenly shattered. His eyes blazed and he brought his fist down on the desk in front of him with such force that it made both Bea and Mrs Minniver jump.

'Don't play games with me, you silly little girl!' he said. His voice now was as hard and cold as a steel trap. 'I'm giving you one last chance. Tell me what you were up to yesterday and this interview could still end without anyone getting hurt. But if you don't, then I promise you, the consequences will be very grave indeed. I should think carefully before you give me your answer. What exactly did you do after you left the games pavilion yesterday?'

'I went for a walk because I had a headache.'

Mr Appollyon raised his right hand and for a moment she thought he was going to strike her. But he made a visible effort to control himself, closing his hand and bringing it slowly down to his side. Bea heard Mrs Minniver let out her breath.

'Very well,' he said, speaking now with his former calmness. 'Have it your own way.'

He stood up and turned to Mrs Minniver. 'Wait here with her until I come back,' he ordered.

After he had left the room, Bea briefly considered appealing to Mrs Minniver's good nature. She had always struck Bea as a fair-minded person. But a brief glance at the headteacher's appalled expression convinced her otherwise. So the two of them waited in a silence broken only by the ticking of the clock above the door.

When Mr Appollyon returned he appeared to be in a much better humour. 'Mrs Minniver, you may return to your work,' he announced. 'I apologise for taking up so much of your time.' He smiled graciously at her. Then he turned to Bea. 'Beatrice, please come with me. There's something I'd like to show you.'

Bea got up and followed him out of the office, wondering what had happened to replace the cold, hard fury he had displayed earlier with this brittle cheerfulness. Out in the corridor, two security guards were waiting. Each took hold of one of her arms.

'I have asked the security officers to accompany us, just as a precaution,' Mr Appollyon told her. 'As long as you cooperate, and don't try to do anything silly like run off, there will be no need for them to get rough. Now follow me.' It soon became clear that he was leading her out of the school altogether.

'Where are we going?' Bea demanded.

Mr Appollyon smiled again but it was a smile that barely sought to disguise a depth of menace. 'The trouble with you, Beatrice, is that you ask too many questions,' he told her. 'However, I think I might have found a way to cure you of that.'

'I want to see my mum and dad,' Bea told him.

Mr Appollyon looked unimpressed. 'You'll see them soon enough,' he replied, 'though they may not be so keen to see you.'

They continued along the path, heading towards the main building of the asylum. Bea had thought herself frightened when she sat in the office and faced the director's furious questions, but now she was completely terrified. She looked into the faces of the security guards, but they were without expression, as if they were not even human.

They entered the main building through a door in the West Wing that Bea had never noticed before, and began to make their way through a network of corridors. They were in the oldest part of the building. The lights were dimmer. Here and there, ancient medical instruments were displayed in dusty glass cases. After a while they halted outside a door; Mr Appollyon took a key out of his pocket and unlocked it.

Immediately inside was a narrow set of stairs and at the top of the stairs Bea was propelled into a small wedge-shaped room. Windows at the wider end looked down on another room, at a lower level. Clearly, this was an observation room; it overlooked a place that Bea had often heard described but had never expected to see: the Shock Room.

There were a number of people in the Shock Room – three senior doctors, two blue-coated orderlies and a patient strapped to the table. As one of the doctors moved to the side, Bea saw, with a lurch of her heart, that the patient was Dante. His head had been shaved and electrical terminals had been connected to his skull. Something had been placed in his mouth to force his jaws apart, and she could tell from his wide, staring eyes that he was petrified.

Mr Appollyon sat down behind a desk. 'It looks like we're just in time,' he said.

'Leave him alone!' Bea shouted.

But no one took any notice of her. The two security guards forced her to sit in a chair, never once letting go of her arms.

'Please,' she begged Mr Appollyon. 'He doesn't deserve this.'

Mr Appollyon frowned. 'People who go about pretending to have dreams after they have come of age are very sick indeed. And sick people require treatment.'

'I'll tell you everything you want to know,' Bea promised.

Mr Appollyon nodded. 'Of course you will. There was never any doubt about that.' Then he turned away and, leaning forward, spoke into a microphone on the desk. 'This is Mr Appollyon. You may go ahead with the treatment now.'

In the Shock Room one of the doctors pressed a switch. Instantly, Dante began writhing and thrashing about on the table, like someone in the grip of a seizure. It may only have taken a few seconds but it seemed to Bea to last for an eternity. Then it was all over and he lay as still as death.

Mr Appollyon turned to Bea. 'That, my dear Beatrice, was a mild dose. I sincerely hope we won't have to increase it, but that all depends on you. Are you going to be completely honest with me now?'

Bea could not trust herself to speak. Instead, she nodded. There was a word for what she had witnessed, a word she had only heard used in her history lessons to describe the barbaric practices of mankind before the Establishment of Permanent Peace: torture. She felt as if she might be sick at any moment.

Mr Appollyon turned to the security guards. 'Wait outside,' he told them.

When they were alone, Bea told him everything: her dreams, her conversations with Dante and their plan to speak to Ezekiel Semiramis. Mr Appollyon's eyes widened when she described how she had eavesdropped from inside the cupboard.

'What exactly did Mr Semiramis say to you after I left the room?' he demanded.

'He didn't want to talk to me at first. He thought it was a trick to get information out of him.'

'But you convinced him otherwise?'

'I tried to. I explained that I was a friend of Dante's and I wanted to know about the ruined city.'

'And what was his answer?'

Bea felt absolutely certain that she should not reveal this to Mr Appollyon but she did not want Dante to suffer any more shock treatment. She would have to make sure that what she said was entirely convincing.

'He said that everyone wanted to know about the ruined city.'

Mr Appollyon looked dissatisfied. 'Is that all? Surely you must have found out more than that? It hardly seems worth the risk you ran.'

'He said he'd come to Tarnagar of his own free will and he would leave in the same way. And it looks as if he was right about that, doesn't it?'

Mr Appollyon ignored her question, but his eyes betrayed a flicker of irritation. Bea realised that she would have to be very, very careful not to provoke him any further.

'Did he tell you why he was so keen to talk to Dante?'

'No.'

'Remember, I have only to speak into this microphone and my colleagues in the room below us will administer another course of treatment to your friend and this time they will not be so gentle.'

'I've told you absolutely everything,' Bea insisted. 'The whole thing was a waste of time. I only wanted to know about the ruined city and he didn't tell me anything.'

'That's because there is no ruined city,' Mr Appollyon told her. 'It's a myth. Do you know what a myth is?'

Bea nodded.

'Of course you do, or so you think. Myths are something we don't talk about any more, just as we don't talk about our dreams, at least not in polite society. Well, I am beyond polite society. I am charged with the security of this island and, unlike you, I may choose which laws and customs to obey and which to break. So I will tell you what a myth really is. It's a lie that has been created to explain something people do not properly understand. And at its heart there is a poison, deadly to our society. Do you know what that poison is? You shake your head but you do know, for you have imbibed some of it yourself, Beatrice, you and your friend Dante. You have allowed yourself to swallow a few tiny drops of it and that is the reason why you are sitting here in front of me today and the reason Dante is strapped to a bed in the room below us.'

'I don't know what you mean,' Bea told him.

'I'm talking about hope. That is the poison at the heart of every myth, hope that there might be some hidden magic that has escaped the attention of the world, hope that you might be able to use this magic to set yourself free, hope that there might be a place where you can escape to, a place where everyone will welcome you, a place where you will be among friends. I'm right, aren't I? That's exactly what you've been guilty of, isn't it? You've allowed yourself to believe in hope.'

Bea stared at him in disbelief. It was as if he had read her mind.

He smiled back at her. 'You see, Beatrice,' he continued. 'It is just as I told you. I can see what you are thinking. I can look into your very soul.'

A DEEPER SILENCE

Dante woke to find himself lying on a bed in a cell. His head was throbbing and his body ached all over, as if he had been beaten. His eyes felt as though sand had been rubbed into them and he could taste blood in his mouth. He sat up with difficulty and discovered that his left leg was manacled to the wall.

After a few moments, an intense feeling of nausea seized him. He leaned over and vomited into the bucket that had been placed beside his bed. There was very little in his stomach and it was soon emptied, but the spasms continued until he was coughing up green bile.

Wiping his mouth on his sleeve, he tried to remember what had happened. At first he could recall nothing, then, gradually, his memory began to return: the guards bursting into the kitchen, seizing him without a word of explanation and dragging him off to the Shock Room, the buzz of the clippers as his head was shaved, the leather restraints that bit into his arms and legs as they strapped him to the table, the taste of the gag that they forced between his teeth, the terrible fear of what was to come next and then…nothing.

He was a patient now, just like his mother. It made him think of the insects that Jerome kept in a glass jar on a window ledge. That was what he had become: a specimen.

He guessed that it must now be the middle of the night. At any other time the sounds of the asylum would have reached even this isolated corridor. But his cell was utterly noiseless – as if he had been buried alive. He felt dreadfully thirsty but there was nothing for him to drink – he knew that this was what his life would be like from now on.

Time passed. Minutes? Hours? It was impossible to say. But then something changed. It was as if the silence that surrounded him became deeper, as if the world itself had come to a halt. Suddenly he heard the sound of a key being turned in the lock and the door slowly began to open.

Panic took hold of him. Were they coming to take him back to the Shock Room? He opened his mouth to scream, but as the door opened fully he saw, to his complete bewilderment, Ezekiel Semiramis standing before him.

'I have come to release you,' Ezekiel told him. He quickly crossed the room and, taking a key from his pocket, unlocked the manacle on Dante's leg. 'Are you all right?' he asked.

Dante nodded, too astonished to ask questions. 'I think so.'

'Can you walk?'

'I don't know.'

'Try.'

Dante felt shaky but he willed himself to take a step.

'Follow me,' Ezekiel told him. 'And try to move as quickly as you can.'

He stepped outside and Dante followed but, to his alarm, a guard was on duty at the end of the corridor. He shrank back against the wall – yet Ezekiel seemed quite unconcerned.

'There is no need to be frightened,' he said, 'the guard can neither see nor hear us.'

'What do you mean?'

'Exactly what I say. Just come with me.'

Ezekiel walked towards the guard, who continued to stand at the end of the corridor, staring into space as if he had been turned into a statue. Ezekiel turned and beckoned to Dante.

'Hurry,' he said. 'We have no time to waste.'

Still dazed and astonished, Dante began to follow Ezekiel along the corridor. At any moment he expected the guard to turn and order them to stop but even when they were right beside him, the guard ignored them, remaining frozen.

'What's happened to him?' Dante asked as they hurried past.

'Nothing has happened to him,' Ezekiel replied. 'Despite the stories people tell about me, I do not believe in harming anyone unless I am forced to.'

'But why is he standing there like that?'

'Because I have stepped outside everyday reality and taken you with me,' Ezekiel told him. 'But I cannot sustain it forever so, please, let us waste no more time talking.'

Ezekiel led him along silent corridors. Occasionally they encountered more guards but all of them stood stock-still. One man appeared to be in the act of scratching his head, another was in mid-yawn. Neither of them so much as blinked as Ezekiel and Dante hurried by. As they left the inmates' cells behind and began to make their way through the area where the senior doctors had their offices, they came across a group of white-coated medical staff, standing in the middle of the corridor. Dante stopped in his tracks as he recognised the doctor who had supervised his treatment earlier that afternoon, but Ezekiel took his arm and drew him onwards.

'Remember, they can neither see nor hear us,' he said. 'All the same, it's best not to touch them. It is only my will that holds us outside time. If we disturb things too greatly they will begin to move once more.'

Even so, it was not easy to slip past the doctors because there was a large group of them standing right in the middle of the corridor. They had clearly been having an animated discussion. Ezekiel flattened himself against the wall and squeezed past. Dante did the same.

'In a moment we will be outside,' Ezekiel told him as they continued down the corridor. 'Then you must take the lead.'

'Me?'

'Yes, of course. I need you to show me where I can find your friend, the one who dreams of the ruined city.'

A GAME OF CARDS

Bea felt as if she had just woken from sleep. The last thing she could remember was standing at the window staring out at the moonlit grounds, feeling utterly miserable and wishing desperately that there was something she could do to help Dante. She had tried to go to sleep but every time she closed her eyes she kept on seeing him – strapped to the bed, his head shaved, his pupils dilated with fear. The horrific picture had been burned into her memory and would not go away.

After her confession, she had glimpsed Dante being wheeled away from the Shock Room before Mr Appollyon had summoned the security guards to take her back to the school.

'What's going to happen to him now?' she had asked.

Mr Appollyon had waved one hand in the air dismissively. 'As I have already explained,' he told her, 'Dante is a very sick boy. We shall have to keep him under constant observation.'

'Does that mean you'll lock him up?'

'Naturally.'

'But you promised to let him go!'

Mr Appollyon looked bored. 'I promised nothing. You know you really are a very tiresome girl, Beatrice.

I think it might be in everyone's best interests to bring your coming-of-age ceremony forward by a couple of weeks.'

Then he had ordered the guards to bring her back to school. They had marched her out of the asylum, retracing the route she had taken less than an hour earlier. It was bizarre, returning to lessons as if nothing unusual had happened. Her classmates regarded her with even greater suspicion now but no one dared ask what Mrs Minniver had wanted.

When she got home from school she found her mother waiting for her.

'Mr Appollyon sent for your father and me this afternoon,' she began, as soon as Bea was inside the door. 'He told us what you've been doing and we were both deeply ashamed. You've let us down badly, Bea. You've brought disgrace upon the family. We will never recover from this.'

'I'm sorry.'

'It's far too late to be sorry. The damage is done.'

Bea thought about telling her mother what she had witnessed that afternoon. She thought about using the word: torture. But her mother would only insist that whatever course of action Mr Appollyon had seen fit to adopt was undoubtedly the right thing to do.

'I'm not sure you realise how close you've come to having yourself declared insane, Bea,' her mother went on. 'One more episode like this and that's what will happen to you. Neither I nor your father will be able to protect you.'

'I know.'

Her mother sighed. 'You were such a well-behaved girl when you were little. Now look at you. Still, at least you won't be seeing any more of that kitchen boy.'

'His name's Dante.'

'I don't care what his name is. He's a menace.'

'He's just a boy, Mum.'

This remark seemed to infuriate her mother. She seized Bea by the arm and shook her. 'He's a dangerous lunatic, Bea! For goodness' sake try and get that through your thick skull.'

'You're hurting me!' Bea exclaimed.

Her mother let go of her arm. 'Better a sore arm than the inside of a cell for the rest of your life! Thank goodness they've brought forward your coming-of-age ceremony, that's all I can say.'

As soon as she had eaten, Bea went to her bedroom in the hope of avoiding her father. But when he arrived home an hour later, he came up to her room and sat on the corner of the bed looking tired and bewildered.

'Why are you doing this, Bea?' he asked in his most reasonable voice.

In some ways this was harder to take than her mother's anger. She found herself wanting to tell him everything.

'You know you're in danger of throwing away everything we've worked for,' he continued. 'Why would you want to do that?'

'That's not what I want,' she replied.

'Then why have you been behaving in this self-destructive way?'

She saw the confusion in his eyes and would have liked to help him understand. Was it possible? After all, he had dared to break the rules himself once.

'I'm not happy, Dad,' she said.

He frowned. 'Happiness is an illusion. Do you know what an illusion is?'

'Yes. It's like a myth.'

He looked startled. 'Myths are something that are best not talked about.'

'Mr Appollyon talked to me about them.'

'Oh well, I suppose that's all right then.'

She felt her sympathy for him begin to evaporate. 'Mr Appollyon and I had quite a long conversation, actually,' she told him. 'He also said that the laws of polite society don't apply to him.' She thought her father might be shocked to hear this but he did not even seem surprised.

'I don't suppose they do,' he agreed.

'But that can't be right, can it?' Bea went on. 'Surely the rules of society ought to apply to everyone, whatever their position.'

Her father shook his head. 'Dr Sigmundus says that society is answerable to authority; authority is not answerable to society.'

'Oh well, if Dr Sigmundus says so, it must be right.'

Her father interpreted the remark literally. He managed a weak smile. 'That's more like it,' he said. 'Stick to the teachings of Dr Sigmundus and you can't go wrong.'

After her father left, she lay on her bed for hours as the world grew darker, going over and over the dreadful events of the last few days, wondering what would have happened if she had done this or that differently. Eventually, she got undressed and climbed into bed, not even bothering to wash or brush her teeth. She lay there waiting for sleep, willing the dark tide of forgetfulness to wash away her emotions. But sleep would not be summoned, so she went and stood at the window, staring out at the moon riding high on a sea of broken clouds.

Suddenly, without her even being aware of it, her mind seemed to release its hold on the tangled net of memories and emotions she had been hauling around with her all day. For a brief instant it was all gone – the pain, the terror and the guilt. And then it came roaring back again. She could not explain what had happened, but she felt that there had been some sort of discontinuity in her life, a break in the line of her being.

As she struggled to understand what it meant, she caught sight of two people standing in the garden looking up at her. They had just suddenly appeared. How was that possible? She restrained an urge to cry out.

As if he knew what she was thinking, Ezekiel Semiramis put his finger to his lips. Then he beckoned for her to come down. With her thoughts in a whirl, she turned from the window, went downstairs in her nightdress and opened the back door.

She wanted to talk to Dante right away, to say how sorry she was for what had happened, to ask whether he was all right, but it was Ezekiel who addressed her.

'We are leaving this place,' he said. 'We have come to offer you the chance to join us.'

'Where are you going?'

'To the ruined city.'

'Then it isn't a myth?'

'It is as real as this island. More so in many ways. But there is no time for discussion now. If you want to come with us, you must leave this instant.'

Bea hesitated. One part of her badly wanted to say yes, to walk out into the night with Ezekiel Semiramis and Dante and shut the door on her old life forever. But she had thrown in her lot with Dante so far and where had it got her? She thought about the way that Mr Appollyon had looked at her as she sat in the headteacher's office trying pathetically to defy him. If she got into trouble again he would not hesitate to place her in Tarnagar's darkest cell.

'Hurry!' Ezekiel urged her. 'I can feel the strength beginning to drain from me.'

'I'm so...so scared,' she told him.

He nodded. 'Of course you are. Anyone who stands on Tarnagar and does not feel their blood turn to ice is not truly alive. Listen to me: you can stay here in this twilight world for the rest of your life or you can breathe the air of freedom. The choice is yours. But we can wait no longer. You must decide now.'

Bea turned from Ezekiel's solemn gaze to look at

156

Dante. There were dark rings under his eyes, and with his shaved head, he looked older than the boy she had met in the woods. She remembered how his body had convulsed on the shock table.

'I'm coming with you,' she declared.

She made her way back to her room as quickly as caution would allow, put on her clothes and crept downstairs. Then, without another word, they all set off through the grounds. She expected them to keep to the shadows wherever possible, but Ezekiel Semiramis led them straight across the lawns where anybody looking out of a window might have seen them. At any moment Bea expected to hear someone call out, but no sound broke the silence. Indeed, it seemed that the night was exceptionally still, as if the world were holding its breath while they fled.

Once they were under cover of the trees, she felt better, but Ezekiel did not relax his pace. He was following an unseen path towards the Outer Wall. She had seen that wall often enough and knew that it surrounded the whole asylum and presented a formidable barrier, over four metres high with razor wire on the top and guard posts at regular intervals.

Suddenly Ezekiel stopped and seemed to shudder.

'What's the matter?' Dante asked him.

He let out a long breath. 'I can hold us outside the world no longer,' he said. 'Now it is only a matter of time before they discover that one or the other of you is missing.'

Suddenly the world around them sprang back to life. The stillness of the night was replaced by the usual background murmur: the rustling of leaves, the hooting of an owl, the sound of some night-creature scurrying in the bushes. Why had these sounds not been audible before? There were so many questions Bea would have liked to ask but she held her tongue and concentrated instead on controlling the sense of panic that was threatening to take hold of her as they set off through the trees at an even faster pace.

Beside her, Dante was fighting exhaustion. The pain in his head was like a red hot needle sticking into his left temple and every part of his body ached. He was wondering how much longer he could carry on when he glimpsed the dark shape of the Outer Wall. They would have to cross this barrier somehow. But the guards who manned the wall were the élite security force. They carried guns, not just the heavy truncheons that their colleagues inside the asylum relied on, and it was well known that they had been instructed to shoot to kill if necessary. Dante felt a huge sense of powerlessness overwhelm him.

Ezekiel came to a halt under the cover of some trees and Dante fully expected him to tell them they would have to turn back, but he displayed the same calm authority he had shown ever since his arrival in Dante's cell.

'Listen to me,' he began. 'Through these trees is the main gate. It is guarded by three security officers who will not hesitate to kill us if they believe we are trying to escape. But there is no need to be alarmed because they will not see us. I am going to put us beyond the world's attention once again.'

'What does that mean?' Bea asked.

'I cannot explain now, except to say that it will seem to you as if the world has stopped. You must have complete faith in me. Will you do that?' His pale blue eyes sought out Bea's and, despite her fear, she nodded.

'Good. Now what I have to do requires enormous concentration and I have only the strength to maintain it for a very brief time. Do exactly what I tell you and keep within my sight at all times. That is absolutely essential. Once we are through this gate it is only a short distance to the coast where a boat is waiting.'

His words seemed to echo in Bea's head and, to her surprise, she felt a faint pang of regret. She hated the island from the depths of her soul but the idea of cutting herself off from everything and everyone she had ever known was a daunting one.

She thought about her parents. She had not got on well with them for a long time but perhaps they had done their best for her. She put her hand to the necklace of beads she wore around her neck. It had been a present from her father for her twelfth birthday. Who would care about her birthdays once she had left the island behind?

While she was thinking this, Ezekiel's expression changed as he began to search deep inside himself for some hidden strength. For the briefest of instants, the air around them seemed to shimmer, then suddenly the

159

deep stillness that Bea had noticed earlier lay all around them once again, enfolding them like a cloak of darkness.

Ezekiel turned back to face them. 'Now,' he said.

The security post was an ugly concrete building, squatting at the base of the wall like a toad sitting beside a fence. Next to it were the great steel gates that could be opened only by the guards inside the building. As they walked towards it, Bea felt naked and defenceless. But they strode right up to the entrance and no one challenged them. Pure terror took hold of Bea as Ezekiel opened the door and stepped inside. She braced herself for the sound of gunfire. Dante went in next and from somewhere within herself she found the courage to follow him.

In the centre of the room four guards sat around a table. They were frozen in the middle of a game of cards. Ezekiel walked calmly across the room towards a key which hung on a hook set in the wall.

Perhaps it was the closeness of the guards, perhaps it was the sight of the guns that lay carelessly beside them or perhaps it was the thought that freedom was now so very close. Whatever the reason, Bea felt the tension in the room becoming unbearable and, without even thinking what she was doing, she clutched at her necklace for comfort, twisting it between her fingers. Suddenly the string broke and beads scattered all over the floor! Ezekiel turned sharply and once more the air seemed to shimmer. Immediately the guards seated at the table gazed around them in confusion.

Horrified, Bea and Dante turned to look at Ezekiel who remained perfectly still. Ignoring the soldiers, he took a deep breath, focused his mind, and once again the world came to a stop.

'I'm sorry,' Bea told him. She felt as if she might faint at any moment. 'Shall I pick them up?'

'Leave them!' Ezekiel told her. 'There is no time!' He spoke like a man struggling for breath. Sweat stood out on his forehead as he led them back outside, towards a smaller door set within the steel gates. He opened this with the key he had taken and, for the first time in their lives, Dante and Bea stepped outside the grounds of the asylum.

'Run!' Ezekiel commanded and together they set off down the road as fast as they could.

Ahead of them they could see the sea and the rugged cliffs that projected out into the water on either side of the bay. It was a sight that neither Dante nor Bea had ever seen before and on any other occasion they might have stopped to gaze in awe at the vast expanse of grey-green water, flecked with white where the waves rolled in relentlessly. But there was no time for that now as Ezekiel led them off the main road, down a path that led steeply through scrubland to a narrow, rocky beach where a boat was anchored some way out to sea.

On the shore a little wooden rowing skiff had been drawn up and after Ezekiel had pushed it out into the water, they climbed on board. Ezekiel took the oars and began to row while Dante and Bea sat nervously in the back, uncertain of their balance, intimidated by the water and looking anxiously over their shoulders towards the shore.

It seemed to take a very long time to cover the distance to the boat but at last they were alongside it. Then it was a matter of taking hold of the ladder that hung down the side and stepping out of the rowing boat that bobbed about like a cork every time anyone shifted their weight. When at last all three had clambered aboard, they wasted no time starting up the engine. As the boat began to move away, Dante wanted to shout for joy. But before he could utter a sound the harsh clatter of an alarm rang out from the darkness behind them.

Part Two
MOITEERA

The cloud-capped towers, the gorgeous palaces,
The solemn temples, the great globe itself,
Yea all which it inherit, shall dissolve
And like this insubstantial pageant faded
Leave not a rack behind. We are such stuff
As dreams are made on, and our little life
Is rounded with a sleep.

William Shakespeare,
THE TEMPEST

'They'll follow us,' Dante said, miserably. 'We'll never be able to outrun them.' He had often heard people in the kitchen talking about the launches that were used to bring goods from the mainland and he knew they were many times more powerful than the boat in which they now stood.

Ezekiel shook his head. 'I very much doubt it,' he said, with a smile. 'I took the precaution of scuppering their boats.'

Bea looked at him incredulously. 'Does that mean we've really escaped?' she asked.

'For the time being, perhaps. Dante is right, of course: they will come after us; but not before we have reached the ruined city. Now I think it would be best if you rest – both of you. There are beds in the cabin below deck.'

Bea would have liked answers to the questions that were filling her head, but she felt as if she had not slept properly for weeks. So she followed Ezekiel down the steps into the galley. He led the way to the back of the boat and opened a door to reveal a compact cabin, with just enough space for a couple of beds on either side, and a cupboard set between them.

Dante lay down immediately on the left-hand bed without even bothering to take off his shoes. He shut his eyes, and within minutes he was asleep. Bea took a little longer. First she took off the jacket she was wearing, as well as her shoes and socks, then she slipped beneath the blankets. She closed her eyes and lay on her back waiting for sleep to come, but her mind was still full of that terrifying moment in the security post when they had come within a whisker of being caught. And it would all have been her fault! She shuddered at the thought and, turning on her side, focused her mind instead on the regular throbbing of the boat's engine. A little while later she, too, was fast asleep.

When she woke she saw that Dante's bed was already empty. She yawned, stretched and got out of bed, making her way unsteadily through the galley and up the steps that led onto the deck. Stepping outside, she was shocked by how cold it had become. The boat was surrounded by a blanket of thick white mist, making it impossible to see more than a metre or two in any direction. What struck her almost as forcibly was the eerie silence, broken only by the chugging of the boat's engine and the occasional harsh cry of a sea bird.

'Weird, isn't it?' Dante said. He was wearing a dark green oilskin with the hood pulled up, and at first she scarcely recognised him.

'I've never seen fog like this before,' she told him.

'Neither have I. You'd better put a coat on or you'll be soaked through in no time. There's a selection downstairs in one of the cupboards.'

168

He was right. Already her clothes felt wet, fine beads of moisture were clinging to her hair, and she was beginning to shiver from the cold. She went back down into the galley and rummaged around in the cupboards until she found a coat that fitted her.

Ezekiel was standing next to Dante when she returned. He gave her one of his tight smiles. 'Did you sleep well?' he asked.

'Yes, thanks.'

'Good. Come and meet our pilot.'

They made their way to the wheelhouse near the front of the boat where a great bear of a man with curly hair and a dense black beard was crouched over the controls.

'This is Manachee,' Ezekiel told her.

'Pleased to meet you.' Bea put her hand out politely.

Manachee grinned and extended his own hand which was at least twice the size of hers.

'Manachee does not believe in wasting words,' Ezekiel told her. 'He prefers to let his actions speak for him. But don't worry. You can trust him entirely. And he's a first-class pilot. Even when no one else can find a way through the fog, Manachee can be relied upon to get us back safely. Now, I expect you could do with some breakfast. Shall we go back to the galley?'

When they were below deck again, Ezekiel opened one of the cupboards and took out some bread and cheese. Dante and Bea were so hungry that it felt like a feast. At first they sat at the table sharing their meal in silence but, once they had eaten, the

169

questions could be put off no longer.

'I don't understand what happened back there on Tarnagar,' Bea said. 'What did you do to the guards to make them stay frozen like that?'

'I will try to explain,' Ezekiel told her. 'But it's a very long story and before I start there is a great deal you have to unlearn.'

'What's that supposed to mean?' Bea demanded.

'Let's begin with what you've already been told,' Ezekiel replied. 'Once upon a time everyone in the world was troubled by desires for things they could not achieve and the result was crime, violence and war. Isn't that how it goes?'

Bea nodded. This was one of the first lessons any child learned in school.

'No society could solve these problems,' Ezekiel continued, 'until the great Dr Sigmundus developed Ichor, the medicine that cured people of their discontent and allowed men and women to be happy with the world as they found it. That's what it says in your text books, right? Well it isn't true. For one thing, it paints a very one-sided picture of the way our country used to be. It leaves out all the beauty, kindness, humour and originality.'

'So you're saying the world wasn't full of crime and violence before Ichor?' Bea asked.

'No, I'm not saying that,' Ezekiel told her. 'What I'm trying to say is that danger is the price of freedom and without the possibility of doing evil, you can never truly do good. So although in the past people suffered from the effects of crime, it was a far healthier society because people were free.'

Bea remained unconvinced. 'Then why do our history books tell a different story?' she asked.

'Because history has been rewritten on the orders of one man: Stanislaus Sigmundus.'

'Then what's the true story?'

'The true story,' Ezekiel replied, 'began many years ago in the city of Ellison. You are quite correct when you say that crime was a major problem in the past and one government after another had struggled to defeat it by conventional means, never with complete success. Finally, they began to look for alternative ways of tackling the problem. That was when the Institute for the Study of the Human Condition was set up in Ellison. Its purpose was to discover what it was about human beings that produced these anti-social urges, and to suggest entirely new methods of dealing with them. Its director was one of the most brilliant scientists our society has ever known. Her name was Yashar Cazabon.'

Dante gasped.

Ezekiel nodded. 'Yes, your mother. That is why I risked everything to find you.'

Dante stared at him in amazement. 'But...but...my mother was a lunatic,' he stammered.

Ezekiel shook his head. 'No Dante, your mother was a very great woman and under her direction the institute began to make some remarkable discoveries, particularly in the area of Odyllic Force.'

'What's Odyllic Force?' Bea asked.

'Odyllic Force is the energy that underlies the fabric of reality. It's invisible, intangible but it is everywhere, flowing through living creatures, swirling about us at all times. Everything that you see around you is, at its most basic level, no more than a concentration of that force. Yashar believed that all those anti-social urges that cause people to commit criminal acts are simply the result of imperfections or distortions in their personal Odyllic fields which could be remedied. That was what she was working on when Sigmundus struck.'

'What did he do?' Dante demanded.

'Sigmundus was supposed to be her assistant,' Ezekiel continued, 'though he was older than her and more experienced. So from the start there was rivalry. He had his own agenda. While your mother was pursuing her investigations into Odyllic Force, Sigmundus was conducting research in a much more conventional area – altering behaviour through the use of drugs. At the same time he was developing powerful political connections. When the time was right, he contacted his friends in the government and accused your mother of treason. She was placed under house arrest and the institute was closed down.

'But she had powerful friends of her own who managed to get her released. She was sent into exile in Moiteera, the city to which we are sailing, where Sigmundus wrongly believed she would be unable to cause any further trouble. He himself, was invited to become a member of the government. He was given responsibility for law and order – a miscalculation by fools who thought they could control him. Within a matter of months he had locked up the very people who invited him into the government. Soon there was no more talk of a government, only of a leader.'

'Didn't anybody try to stop him?' Dante asked.

'Of course they did. But Sigmundus was absolutely ruthless. Those who opposed him were imprisoned, tortured or executed. When the city of Moiteera rose up against him, Sigmundus used poison gas to kill its inhabitants.'

'Is that the ruined city I keep dreaming about?' Bea asked.

'Yes. No one knows how many thousands of people died. Nevertheless, people continued to resist his rule. But he had expected that. Violence and brutality were only short-term solutions. While he was working at the institute he had developed a much more effective way of controlling people.'

'Ichor?' Dante suggested.

'Exactly. At first he planned to add it to the water supply but he quickly abandoned this idea.'

'Why?'

'Because young children who were given the drug became violently disturbed or simply lost all will to live. Many of them ended up as patients in the asylum. It soon became clear that it could only safely be given to people when they had reached a certain age. So the coming-of-age ceremony was developed. And it worked perfectly. Within a short time the struggle against Sigmundus was almost over. Those of us who were still

173

able to resist joined forces and we attempted to halt the production of Ichor.'

'Why didn't you succeed?'

Ezekiel smiled, ruefully. 'Sigmundus has based the entire economy of this country upon the manufacture of Ichor. To the north of Vanna, there are thousands of manufacturing plants working day and night, to process the raw material from the mines. If we sabotaged one plant every day of the year, we would put only a fraction out of use.'

'I still don't see what all this has got to do with what you did to those guards back on Tarnagar,' Bea said, impatiently.

'I'm coming to that,' Ezekiel replied but before he could say any more, Manachee descended the galley steps.

'We are approaching the Dragon's Teeth,' he announced.

Ezekiel nodded. He turned back to Dante and Bea. 'I'm afraid we shall have to suspend our explanations for the time being,' he told them. 'The most dangerous part of our journey lies just ahead of us.'

THE DRAGON'S TEETH

In the last few minutes the air around them seemed to have grown thicker and the light dimmer; but at the same time the colours of everything appeared more intense, lit up from within. Dante looked at Ezekiel and saw that something peculiar was happening to his face. His features had begun melting and rearranging themselves, taking on an altogether different, more sinister expression so that there was something wolfish about him. Alarmed, Dante turned to Bea, only to see that her eyes looked wild and feral, like a cornered animal's, and her lips were stretched back over her teeth. He had the distinct impression that she was readying herself to pounce, and a tide of fear rushed through his body. What had happened to his companions?

'Do not be afraid,' Ezekiel told him, but his voice had a hollow echo, as if he were speaking from the bottom of a well. 'Whatever you are seeing now is merely the effect of disturbances in the Odyllic field. Once we have passed through this area, everything will return to normal.'

But there was something about his voice that suggested he was putting on an act, pretending to be concerned about their welfare while all the time laughing at them in secret.

Dante glanced down at the table, and saw that the surface of the wood was swarming with shapes and patterns like living creatures, changing their form from one moment to the next. He peered more closely. Now it seemed that he was looking at writing. He felt convinced that some important message was being revealed to him, if only he could understand; a moment later he was equally certain that what he saw was really a series of pictures telling a story – something about a boy on a boat travelling across the sea. Suddenly he understood that the boy was himself and the pictures were no more than his own thoughts projected onto the surface of the table.

'What's happening to us?' Bea asked. There was terror in her voice, and when Dante looked up he saw not a wild animal, but a small child, no more than five or six years old. How had he mistaken her for an animal? But even as he looked she began to change again, ageing before his eyes until he was gazing at an old woman. Her hair was grey, her teeth broken and she was staring at him with a look of terrible sadness. Why did she look so sad? Was it because they had once been young, both of them, a long, long time ago? Perhaps they had been friends then? Yes, he remembered now. They had sailed on a ship together across a sea of fog, escaping from someone or something that threatened to destroy them.

'Try to remain calm.' A voice interrupted his thoughts.

'All this will pass in a little while.' Dante looked across at the owner of the voice and saw a man who looked like a wolf, a man whose body was full of a fierce power, held in check only by the force of his will. But that will could change at any moment and he could kill them with the greatest of ease, if that was what he chose to do.

'I can't remain calm!' Bea exclaimed. 'I'm losing my mind.'

Her words resonated deeply within Dante. 'She's right,' he thought. 'That's what all this means. And this man who pretends to reassure us, wants us to lose our minds. That's why he brought us onto this boat in the first place.' In desperation, he stood up. 'I'm getting out of here,' he declared. He heard himself speak and thought how feeble and pathetic he sounded.

'There isn't anywhere to go,' the wolf-man told him.

But Dante could hear the mockery in his voice. He's trapped us! he thought. A wave of exhaustion washed over him but he knew he had to fight it. He could not give up now. That was what the wolf-man wanted. He turned back to Bea to see how she was reacting but, to his horror, her hair was writhing with insects. They were swarming all over her head. He opened his mouth to cry out, and at that very moment something seemed to fly across the galley, startling him so that he stumbled backwards.

There it was again: a bat. And now there were more of them, darting back and forth on leathery wings. He could hear their high-pitched cries and yet he had always been told that the cry of a bat was inaudible. What other lies had they told him, he wondered? He put his hands to his head as another bat shot past him and immediately felt the same writhing mass of insect life he had seen crawling upon Bea's scalp. They were consuming him!

'Try to understand that none of what you see is real,' the wolf-man insisted. 'It is only a reflection of your fears. The best thing to do is to sit down and try to relax.'

But Dante was covered with insects and if he did not do something to stop them, they would eat him alive. He stumbled across the galley, ducking to avoid the bats, determined to get up on deck and throw himself into the water. But it was so hard to find the door. The floor, the walls, the ceiling – every surface he looked at – was seething with constantly changing patterns that pulsed and throbbed with energy, and he could hear the sound of that energy, humming and whining in the air around him, giving off flickers of coloured light, like sparks from some great bonfire.

'Where do you think you're going?' It was the wolf-man, standing so close that Dante could feel the heat of his breath.

The wolf-man's eyes were fixed upon him and Dante could neither move nor look away. He wanted to speak, to tell this creature to leave him alone, but his voice would not respond. He had to use all his willpower merely to whisper, 'Up on deck.'

'It isn't wise,' the wolf-man told him.

'You can't stop me!' Dante replied, forcing the words out of his throat.

'I don't intend to,' the wolf-man assured him, 'if that's

178

what you really want to do. But I'm coming with you.'

'So am I,' said Bea. He had not seen her get up and make her way across the room but here she was and to his surprise her head was no longer covered with insects; instead there was a huge gash on her temple and blood was running down her face, onto her neck. While he had been stumbling about looking for the door, the wolf-man had attacked her! They had to get away from him! If only he could find that door!

The wolf-man reached towards him and Dante jumped backwards, expecting a blow to his stomach, but instead the wolf seized the handle of the door – Dante had been standing beside it all the time. As the door opened he was immediately hit by a blast of cold air.

The wolf showed its teeth mockingly. 'Let's go then,' it said.

Cautiously, Dante clambered up the stairs that led onto the deck. He had forgotten about the fog. Now, as he stood on deck, it was clear why the wolf had allowed him to leave the galley. There was no safety up here! The milky-white blanket of mist that surrounded the boat was swirling with hideous shapes: faces leered at him, claws reached out to snatch him and he shrank back from them, cowering in defeat.

The monsters were in the water as well – dreadful creatures with human faces and mouths full of pointed teeth. They were looking at him expectantly, their eyes glittering with greed. He turned back to the wolf.

'Why don't you kill me now?' he demanded.

To his astonishment, the wolf gave a low chuckle.

179

'I have no desire to kill you,' he replied. 'Whatever you are witnessing is no more than the enactment of your fears and anxieties. It may not help you to hear this, but I promise you it's true.'

'My parents are in the water!' Bea suddenly shouted. 'We must help them!'

Dante stared at the grey waves that surrounded the boat. There were so many faces just beneath the surface. Was she right?

The wolf shook his head. 'Your parents are on the island of Tarnagar,' he said.

'Tarnagar!' The name made Dante shudder. Where had he heard it before? Of course! It was where he had lived before finding himself on this boat, where he had walked up and down the stairs carrying trays of food to men and women locked away in cells.

'You don't understand,' Bea said. 'They're out there in the sea. They're calling out for us to help them.' She ran across to the rail and leaned out over the water.

Immediately the wolf followed her and took hold of her arm. 'It's an illusion,' he told her. 'There's nothing out there but water.'

Bea looked at him in furious disbelief. 'I can see them,' she insisted. 'They won't be able to last much longer. I have to try and save them.' She began struggling in his grip.

Dante was confused. Should he help her? But even as he was asking himself this, she suddenly stopped struggling and went entirely limp. Then she let out a long sigh.

'They've gone,' she said.

'They were never there,' Ezekiel told her gently. He turned to Dante. 'Are you feeling better now?' he asked.

To his surprise and great relief, Dante had begun to feel more like himself. He put his hand to his head. There were no insects, just hair. The bats had disappeared and all around him the pulsating patterns were fading away. As quickly as it had taken on such a sinister appearance, everything was now returning to normal.

'I don't understand,' he said.

'We have just passed through the Dragon's Teeth,' Ezekiel told him. 'It is a line of buoys floating across the entrance to the bay of Moiteera. Built into each one is a little invention Yashar developed at the Institute for the Study of the Human Condition. It emits a signal that disrupts the surrounding Odyllic field. As a result, anyone who passes through this area experiences powerful hallucinations.'

'Are you saying that you knew this was going to happen?'

'Yes.'

'And you didn't stop it?'

'It's one of our defences.'

'But we could have jumped over the side,' Dante exclaimed.

'I would have prevented you.'

'You can't be certain of that.'

'Yes I can.' He spoke with complete conviction.

'Well at least you could have warned us.'

181

Ezekiel sighed. 'Any warning I gave you in advance would only have seemed like a threat.'

'So none of what we saw was real?' Bea mused, as much to herself as to anyone else.

'Who's to say what is real?' Ezekiel replied. 'Your parents were not in the water, that's for certain; but it was them you saw, and they are lost to you now as surely as if they had sunk beneath the waves.' He turned to Dante. 'You were frightened of me, were you not?' he asked.

'I thought you were a wolf,' Dante admitted, embarrassed. Now that he put it into words, his fear sounded ridiculous.

Ezekiel smiled. 'It would not be the first time I have been given that name. And perhaps you are wise not to trust me completely, for now at least. In time you may get to know me better.'

'But what were all those patterns I kept seeing everywhere?' Dante asked, anxious to change the subject.

'The lines of force.'

'But I thought you said it was all an illusion.'

Ezekiel shrugged. 'The difference between truth and illusion is not always as simple as people think. Now look, here is our pilot.'

They looked up to see Manachee coming towards them. To Dante's eyes, he looked pale and seemed unsteady on his feet.

'How did you fare in the Dragon's Teeth?' Ezekiel asked him.

'I saw my brother,' Manachee replied.

'Manachee's brother was killed by Sigmundus's troops three years ago,' Ezekiel told them.

'Were you frightened?' Bea asked.

Manachee shook his head. 'It's not the first time I've seen him,' he said.

'What did he say to you?' Ezekiel asked.

'The same as always,' Manachee replied. 'He told me exactly how I would meet my death.'

'But did he tell you when?'

'No.'

'Then let us hope it will not be soon.'

While they had been standing on deck a breeze had sprung up and now at last the mist began to thin out as the wind tore wisps of it away.

'Look,' Bea said, 'there's land up ahead.'

Dante gazed in the direction she had pointed, to where the blurred shape of a coastline was beginning to emerge from the fog.

Ezekiel nodded. 'Soon you will see the city of your dreams,' he told Bea, 'and I will introduce you both to the Púca.'

'Who are they?' Dante asked.

'The Púca are the ones who dwell in the ruins,' Ezekiel replied, 'and they are greatly looking forward to meeting you – at least most of them are.'

AN ARMY OF DREAMERS

It was midday when they finally sailed into the ruined city. The dock was entirely abandoned, but its wharves were still crowded with the rusting hulls of old ships. The mighty warehouses, which must once have bustled with the work of loading and unloading cargo, were silent now and empty. Crates and packing cases lay where they had been abandoned, their contents long ago plundered or scattered by the weather. The great cranes that had once hauled them ashore stood motionless like the skeletons of giant beasts long vanished from the earth.

'Before Sigmundus destroyed it, Moiteera was famous all over the world for its culture and its learning,' Ezekiel informed them when they had tied up the boat and clambered unsteadily ashore. 'Of course for him it was just a centre of resistance that had to be crushed.'

An unpleasant thought occurred to Bea as they made their way along the dockside. 'What happened to all the people?' she asked. 'I mean, if they were poisoned like you said, surely they would have died where they stood and we'd see...'

'Their bones lying everywhere?' Ezekiel suggested.

'Yes, I suppose that's what I meant.'

'The soldiers removed all the bodies and buried them in mass graves outside the city. In those days Sigmundus was not quite as sure of himself as he later became. He wanted to make certain the evidence was removed from the sight of the world.'

He led them away from the derelict port, through a warren of narrow streets, towards the centre of the city. Once they had left the waterfront behind, the streets became wider and the houses grander.

'These were the homes of wealthy merchants,' Ezekiel told them, pointing to some of the more ostentatious buildings.

The doorways were framed with marble pillars, though often the doors hung drunkenly on one hinge, or lay in splinters on the ground. In almost every window the glass had been smashed but in a few houses ragged curtains still fluttered in the breeze.

'Everything was looted by the soldiers,' Ezekiel explained. 'They took anything they could carry. The rest they destroyed out of sheer vandalism.'

They turned now into a wide street with rows of trees on either side, their branches full of pink blossom. There was something extraordinarily uplifting about the sight of so much beauty in the midst of such desolation.

'This was known as the Boulevard of Lovers,' Ezekiel said. 'Fashionable young men and women would walk up and down this street arm in arm. It was the place to meet your friends and to be seen by others. People used to say that for as long as the trees in the Boulevard of Lovers blossomed, the city of Moiteera would flourish.'

'They were wrong about that then,' Bea observed, sadly.

Ezekiel raised one eyebrow. 'The city is not dead yet,' he told her. 'You will find that out soon enough.'

Halfway down the Boulevard of Lovers, they turned into a side street that led in turn into a square. In the middle of the square was a statue of a man reading from a book. The stone from which it had been carved was white with bird droppings and part of one arm had been broken off but it was still possible to make out the look on the man's face. He was smiling, though there was something sad about his smile, as if he had been told some very grave news and had resigned himself to making the best of it.

'The poet, Alvar Kazimir Mendini,' Ezekiel told them. 'He was the most famous inhabitant of Moiteera.'

On the plinth below the statue were carved some lines from one of his poems. Bea read aloud:

'The man who stands on the platform above the cheering crowd –

Why does he look so listless? Why does his head seem bowed?

Is it because of the emptiness when the cheers begin to fade?

Is it because of the silence at the end of the grand parade?'

'Does he remind you of anyone?' Ezekiel asked.

They looked up at the poet's face again. It seemed to Dante that he had a kind expression and the thought crossed his mind that he would have liked to have

186

known this man, but there was no resemblance to anyone he had ever known.

Suddenly Bea cried out, 'It can't be!'

Ezekiel smiled. 'It's quite obvious really, isn't it?' he said.

'What do you mean?' Dante asked. 'What's obvious?'

'Whose face can you see on the statue, Bea?' Ezekiel asked.

'Dante's,' she whispered.

Dante stared at her in astonishment. Then he looked at Ezekiel. 'Are you telling me...?, he began.

Ezekiel nodded. 'Alvar Mendini was your father, Dante. It was here in Moiteera that your parents met. They were Moiteera's most brilliant and most famous couple.'

'What happened to him?' Dante demanded. 'How did he die?'

'A bomb exploded while he was on his way to the market one day. That was about a year before Sigmundus sent his flying machines to bomb the city with poison gas. In fact, it was the unrest that followed your father's death that brought about his decision to punish the people of Moiteera more severely.'

Dante stood in front of the statue experiencing a mixture of powerful emotions. Pride at his father's achievements, sorrow to think that he would never know him, anger at the treachery that had led to his death.

After they had been standing there for some time in silence, Ezekiel put his hand on Dante's shoulder.

'You can return here as often as you like,' he said, 'but right now there are people waiting for us.'

He led them across the square and along a small street lined with the ruins of what must once have been a parade of small shops, coming out at last into another grand boulevard. Bea stopped and gasped when she saw it, for there was no mistaking the architecture which confronted her. This was the very landscape of her dreams. And for the first time in her life she felt as if she had truly come home.

'We are in the heart of the city now,' Ezekiel told them. He pointed to an imposing building at one end of the street and Bea immediately recognised the cracked and broken steps that led up to the entrance. 'This is our headquarters, for the time being at least, though we never use the same building for very long.'

Dante wondered who he meant by 'we' but he suspected they would find out soon.

The hotel was gloomy inside for there was no electric light. Everything smelt damp and musty. But it was clear from the furnishings that this must once have been a very grand place. The faded plush chairs still waited for the guests to sit down and order their morning coffee, and the bell was still in place at the reception desk where once the new arrivals would have waited to have their bags brought up to their rooms.

As they made their way down the wide marble steps that led to the basement, Ezekiel explained that this had once been the most expensive hotel in Moiteera. 'The chef who worked here was paid as much as the mayor.'

Dante was astonished at this, since on Tarnagar the kitchen staff were the least important people, below even the cleaners. 'What did the mayor think about that?' he asked.

Ezekiel smiled. 'He didn't like it.'

It would have been very dark indeed at the bottom of the stairs had lighted candles not been placed on a table. It was clear that someone was expecting them.

'Who lit the candles?' Dante asked warily.

'You will see in a moment,' Ezekiel replied. He led the way along the corridor to a door above which had been written 'Mendini Room'. 'As you see, the inhabitants of Moiteera had a great respect for literature,' Ezekiel said. He knocked three times on the door. It opened a crack and a face peered out. Ezekiel mumbled something inaudible and the door opened properly. Then they stepped into a large room full of the most strangely dressed people Dante and Bea had ever seen.

'Welcome to the Púca,' Ezekiel announced.

There must have been more than a hundred people in the room, maybe more – men, women and children. They were sitting on chairs, perching on tables, squatting on the floor or leaning against the walls.

On Tarnagar you could always tell what a person did by the clothes they wore. Administrators dressed in grey suits, doctors in white coats, security guards in black uniforms and cleaners in brown overalls. Even children were obliged to follow suit. Bea had worn a black blazer to school every day and Dante had worn the blue-and-red striped tunic of a kitchen worker since he was old enough to walk.

But the Púca seemed to wear whatever they liked and, by the looks of things, the more colourful the better. Nor was that the only unusual thing about them. Unlike the men on Tarnagar, who kept their hair to a uniform length, some of these had hair down to their shoulders while others preferred to shave their heads. Some had beards, others were clean-shaven. Many of them sported intricate tattoos on their arms.

On the whole, they looked friendly enough but unpredictable. As Dante was thinking this, he noticed a young man with long black hair and a beard seated towards the back of the room. Unlike the others, who were all gazing keenly at the newcomers, this man stared blankly in front of him and his face showed not the slightest awareness of anything that was happening. By his side stood a grey-haired woman who rested her hand upon his shoulder. She was dressed plainly, in a long black robe and stared directly at Dante with a gaze that was so intense, he found himself turning away.

The room fell silent now and Ezekiel began to address them. 'Ladies and gentlemen, friends, members of the Púca, you have no idea what a pleasure it is to see you again. You all know where I have been, and why. I can tell you it was not an experience I would care to repeat. However, I am happy to present to you someone whom we had long thought dead – the son of Yashar Cazabon and Alvar Mendini.'

The room erupted! The Púca cheered, stamped their

feet, banged on the tables and whistled. Many of them began calling for a speech. Dante stared back at them in astonishment. He certainly hadn't expected anything like this. It must have been several minutes before the cheering died down.

Ezekiel turned to him. 'Well, Dante,' he said, 'that was quite a welcome. Would you like to say a few words in response?'

All eyes were fixed on him and Dante knew he had to think of something. 'Thank you very much,' he began. 'I've only just begun to find out the truth about my parents. They told me my mother was a dangerous lunatic.' There were cries of indignation when he said this and he could feel tears welling up inside him. 'I'm just so grateful to Ezekiel for rescuing me and making it possible for me to leave Tarnagar forever.' He shook his head, unable to say any more.

Ezekiel intervened to spare him. 'Thank you very much, Dante,' he said. 'I know we are all very excited about having you here among us. And now ladies and gentlemen, I would like to introduce someone else I met on Tarnagar. This is Beatrice Argenti. She has been dreaming about Moiteera for as long as she can remember. And at last she has made it here.'

This time there was polite applause. Then the Púca got to their feet, gathering around Ezekiel and firing questions at him. Many of them also wanted to shake Dante's hand and tell him how much they had admired his parents. Bea stood by herself feeling a little left out until a girl of about her own age came over and introduced herself. She had red hair down to her waist and skin so pale it reminded Bea of the fine china her mother kept on a display shelf in the kitchen.

'I'm Maeve,' she said. 'I imagine you're feeling a bit overwhelmed.'

Bea nodded. 'I am, really,' she said. 'I didn't have any idea what to expect.'

'It must be very strange meeting us all like this,' Maeve agreed, 'but you'll find everyone is very friendly once you get to know them.'

'How long have you lived here?' Bea asked.

'Oh I was born here,' Maeve said. 'My parents are both Púca. That's my mother over there.' She pointed to a woman who had just come into the room carrying a tray of food. She had the same colour hair as Maeve but hers was cut as short as a boy's. 'You've already met my father, Manachee. There aren't too many like me, though,' she added. 'Most people find their way here because they're running away from coming-of-age ceremonies, because they're in trouble with the security officers or just because their path happens to cross Ezekiel's for one reason or another.'

Maeve's mother came over then to ask Bea whether she wanted anything to eat. There was nothing familiar on the tray, but all of it smelled enticing. She chose a kind of pastry and bit into a delicious combination of flavours, dark and pungent with a hint of sweetness at its heart.

'This is wonderful!' she said.

'Well, you've certainly made a good first impression,'

Maeve said when her mother had moved off. 'My mum made those herself.'

On the other side of the room, Ezekiel was introducing Dante to a boy called Albigen. He was a few years older than Dante, tall with light-brown skin, tight curly hair and a lopsided grin. A jagged scar ran across his forehead from just above one eyebrow to the bridge of his nose.

'Albigen will be your Guardian,' Ezekiel told him. 'That means it is his job to look after you until you get to know your way around.'

Dante wasn't sure he liked the sound of this. Growing up in the asylum had taught him to be independent. 'I'll be all right on my own,' he said.

Ezekiel shook his head. 'None of the Púca is ever on his own,' he replied. 'We depend upon each other at all times. That's how we survive.'

Albigen didn't seem put out at Dante's reluctance to accept his services. 'I know how you feel,' he said. 'I was suspicious of everybody when I first got here. That's what the world out there does to you. But you needn't worry. No one's going to start ordering you around, least of all me.'

He went on to tell Dante the story of how he had come to join the Púca. 'I grew up in a city called Vanna. Perhaps you've heard of it?'

Dante nodded.

'Most of the people who live there work in the mines and it's all they ever think about. Both of my parents were miners and it was always assumed I'd follow in their footsteps. But I hated everything about the mines, the smell of them, the way the dust got into your clothes, your hair, even your skin. Besides, I always had this feeling that there was more to life. From as early as I can remember I was asking questions that made my mum and dad nervous. They just used to tell me that everything would fall into place when I started to receive Ichor.'

'But it didn't?'

'Ichor had absolutely no effect on me. I might as well have drunk a glass of water. Of course I didn't dare tell anyone that it wasn't working. I just tried to look content, all the time waiting for someone to find me out. Then one day they did. It wasn't anything in particular I said or did – at least I don't think so. I expect the authorities had been keeping their eye on me for a long time and they finally put two and two together. I was sitting in my class at school, trying to focus on what the teacher was saying when I got summoned to the headteacher's office. When I arrived I found two security guards waiting for me. They didn't speak. I was just shoved into the back of a van and driven away. I thought they were going to kill me and I was thinking about all the things I would never get a chance to do when the van suddenly came to a screeching halt. That was when I was thrown forward and cut my forehead. It was a Púca ambush, of course. I'll never forget seeing Ezekiel's face when he opened the doors of the van and let me out.'

'How did they know you were in there?' Dante asked.

'It's our job to know,' said a red-haired woman carrying a tray of food. 'Have something to eat.'

'Thank you.' Dante regarded the food suspiciously then opted for a slice of plain brown bread.

'Did Ezekiel tell you where we got our name from?' the red-haired woman went on.

'Not yet.'

'That's Ezekiel for you,' the woman said with a grin. 'He never tells you the whole story, just enough to whet your appetite. Well, the Púca is a creature from an ancient story, a kind of goblin if that means anything to you.'

Dante shook his head.

'In the story the Púca goes around making a general nuisance of himself, causing mischief when people aren't looking, shutting doors that should be open and opening doors that should have be shut – that sort of thing. And that's just what we're like. We make as much trouble for Sigmundus and his soldiers as we can. He never sees us come or go but whenever his plans go wrong, he knows we're likely to be at the bottom of it.'

'That was Keeva,' Albigen said when the woman had moved off. 'She's one of the founders – the ones who set up the Púca. She would have known your mother well.'

Dante turned to look at her again. He wished now that he'd spoken to her at greater length.

'Don't worry,' Albigen told him. 'You'll be seeing plenty of us all in the days to come. We're a close-knit community. Joining the Púca is like finding a family you never knew you had.'

They were interrupted by the arrival of the woman in black who had been sitting at the back of the room when Dante arrived.

'So you are Yashar Cazabon's son,' she said. Unlike everyone else he had spoken to so far, she did not sound friendly.

Dante nodded. 'That's me,' he agreed.

'This is Perdita,' Albigen explained. He sounded reluctant to introduce her.

'Pleased to meet you,' Dante told her.

'I'm afraid I cannot return that sentiment,' Perdita replied. 'Your arrival here today has opened up an old wound for me.'

'I'm sorry,' Dante said, puzzled, 'I don't know what you mean.'

'To everyone here your mother was a great person but to me she brought nothing but sorrow.' Her voice was full of bitterness.

'I don't understand,' Dante went on. 'What did she do to you?'

'Look over there, at the back of the room.'

Dante looked in the direction she was pointing and saw the young man with the blank expression. He was still in exactly the same position as he had been when Dante entered the room.

'That is my son, Eugenius,' Perdita continued. 'Before he listened to Yashar he was a happy, smiling boy, full of life. He brought joy to everyone who saw him. Now he can neither speak nor laugh. He doesn't even know where he is. All he does is sit and stare, day after day. If

I didn't dress him like a little child, he would go naked. If I didn't feed him with a spoon he would waste away and die.'

'That's terrible,' Dante agreed. 'But what has it got to do with my mother?'

'Your mother kindled in him a desire to control Odyllic Force. I tried to warn him that it was dangerous but he wouldn't listen. He only had ears for Yashar. Night after night he struggled to reach the Odyll. He forgot about everything else, including his own mother. And one day, it seems, he found the way there. Or perhaps he found somewhere in between that world and this. For he has never come back to tell us. Look at him now. His body is still here but his soul is lost and no one can recall it.'

Her words filled Dante with dismay. Why hadn't Ezekiel warned him about this?

'I have to bathe him, clean him and lead him about like a dog. What will happen to him when I am gone? Tell me that?'

'I don't know,' Dante said.

'Of course you don't! Nobody knows. His body will wither away and die, that much is certain, but what will become of his spirit? That is the gift your mother gave to me, Dante Cazabon, and that is why her son will never be welcome in my eyes.'

Before Dante could say another word, she turned and walked away.

'Take no notice of her,' Albigen said.

'But is what she said true?' As he asked the question

Dante watched Perdita thread her way across the room until she was standing beside her son once again. She bent down to speak to him and took his lifeless hand in hers.

'What she says is true enough,' Albigen told him, 'but it wasn't your mother's fault. Eugenius understood the risk when he joined the Púca. We are at war. Sigmundus wants to destroy us and we have to use every weapon we've got to stay alive. It's the price you have to pay for freedom.'

Dante was taken aback. Even he knew that wars were something from the dark days of history, periods of blood lust, killing and collective insanity. But before he could ask any further questions, Albigen was called away to help with the food.

Dante was still puzzling over their conversation when a group of musicians appeared in the far corner of the room and began to play. Apart from a set of drums, Dante did not recognise any of the instruments. On Tarnagar music was sometimes played on important occasions like the Leader's Day parade. But the music of Tarnagar was brisk and stirring – songs in praise of Dr Sigmundus, tunes that you could march along to, whereas the music of the Púca had no words and there did not even seem to be much of a tune at first. But as Dante listened more carefully, he began to discern a sinuous melody snaking in and out of the rhythm in a complicated, shifting arrangement that made him feel as if he was drifting towards the borders of sleep.

'Enjoying the party?' Bea asked, bringing him

suddenly back from his dreamlike state.

'I suppose that's what it is,' Dante said. 'I've never been to a party before.'

'I have,' Bea told him, 'but never one like this.'

'Have they given you a Guardian?' he asked.

'Yes, a girl called Maeve. That's her, over there, with the red hair.'

'Mine's a boy called Albigen.'

She nodded. 'So do you think that's it then?'

Dante frowned. 'What do you mean?'

'Do we just live happily ever after from now on?'

Dante shook his head. 'I don't think so. Somehow, I think this is just the beginning.'

'The beginning of what, though?'

Dante thought of what Albigen had just been saying. 'The beginning of the war against Sigmundus,' he suggested.

Bea gave him a shocked look. 'Are you serious?'

Dante shrugged. 'That was what Albigen called it.'

Bea cast a critical glance around the room. 'This isn't my idea of an army,' she said.

Just then Ezekiel came over to join them. He must have overheard Bea's remark because he smiled grimly. 'It's an army of dreamers,' he told her. 'And I promise you, there is nothing in the world that our enemy fears more.'

THE VIEW FROM THE TOWER

Dante and Bea were each given a room in the hotel. Dante's was on the second floor and Bea's was on the first. They were ten times the size of the room Dante was used to and full of beautiful antique furniture. In the centre of each room was an enormous four-poster bed with elaborately carved bedposts and a heavy velvet canopy. Separate bathrooms opened off the bedrooms but the taps had long since ceased to function and hot water had to be carried upstairs from the kitchen.

Despite the relative luxury in which he now found himself, Dante had difficulty sleeping at night. He was troubled by a recurring nightmare in which he found himself standing at the top of the Great Tower looking down on the cruel stones far beneath him. His body was weak with fear and his legs shook so much he could hardly stand. But a sense of inevitability drove him to clamber onto the parapet that ran around the edge of the tower. There was a moment of regret as he felt the security of solid ground beneath his feet for the last time. Then he stepped out into the thin air of dawn and began falling through space.

With a cry he would wake, his heart racing and his body bathed in sweat. Relieved to find himself still alive, he would lie there, while his heartbeat gradually returned to normal and his eyes grew used to the moonlight coming through the window. Slowly the sense of panic would subside and eventually he would drift off back to a dreamless sleep.

These night-time fears were matched, to some extent, by his anxieties during the daytime. When would the soldiers come looking for him? What was the explanation for their delay? He would have liked to ask Ezekiel these questions but the Púca's leader was not around much and even when he could be tracked down, his answers were enigmatic and unsatisfactory.

Albigen was more forthcoming. 'Sigmundus will not strike immediately,' he said as they sat beside the pond in the courtyard at the rear of the hotel. Once a fountain had sprung from the mouth of a great bronze dolphin in the middle of the pond and exotic fish had swum in its waters. Now the fountain had run dry, and the surface of the water was covered with a mantle of thick green weed. But the place still possessed a faded beauty and in the early morning sunshine bright blue dragonflies darted through the air like needles of light.

'It's not his way to act in haste,' Albigen continued. 'At least not nowadays. But he won't forget that you have defied him and when he feels the time is right, he will send his forces against us.'

'And what will happen then?' Dante asked.

'He will find himself chasing shadows.'

Bea was less worried about the future than Dante. For her, the immediate problems were more pressing. One of the first things she had done after Maeve had shown her her room had been to run up and down the stairs with bucketloads of water until she had enough to fill the bathtub. The resulting bath had been only lukewarm, but had still felt absolutely marvellous.

Once she was clean, Bea began to face up to the other difficulties her new life presented. To start with she had to adjust to owning nothing more than the clothes she had been wearing when she left Tarnagar. A few days after her arrival, however, Maeve brought her to a warehouse near the docks where the Púca kept supplies of clothing.

'Where did all this stuff come from?' Bea asked in amazement as she stood looking at racks of clothes in different sizes, colours and styles. There were some uniforms she recognised from Tarnagar but many other garments she did not.

'Every so often a unit gets sent out on an action,' Maeve said, enigmatically.

'What sort of action?' Bea asked, holding up a sweater against her and looking in a mirror that had been thoughtfully set up nearby. It suited her, she decided.

'A small group of us mounts a raid on a nearby town.'

'You mean it's stolen?' Bea dropped the sweater in dismay.

'Of course it's stolen,' Maeve replied matter-of-factly.

'Then it's true.'

'What's true?'

'What they taught us at school. That without Ichor the world would degenerate into lawlessness and violence.

People would be afraid to walk the streets because other people would kill them and steal their possessions.'

'We don't kill anyone unless they try to kill us first,' Maeve said disdainfully, 'and we take what we need to keep us alive because we have no alternative.'

'You make it sound so easy.'

Maeve shook her head. 'I had an uncle once,' she told Bea. 'His name was Rory. I used to ride around on his shoulders and he would sing while he carried me.'

'What happened to him?'

'Sigmundus's troops attacked the city. He was on look-out duty. One of the soldiers crept up behind him and cut his throat.'

Bea stared at her in horror.

'It's true,' Maeve nodded. 'Ichor hasn't taken all the violence out of our society, whatever they tell you at school. It just makes people easier to control, that's all.' She picked up the sweater and held it up against Bea. 'It's your colour,' she said. 'You should take it.

Dante did not share Bea's reservations. Everything he had ever owned on Tarnagar had been handed down from someone else – usually because it was nearly worn out already. All his life he'd watched other people being given things he wasn't allowed to have. So a little redistribution of wealth seemed perfectly reasonable to him. But to throw away his striped tunic still felt strange, like sloughing off an old skin.

'What are you going to do with it?' he asked Albigen.

'Burn it,' Albigen told him. 'We need to get rid of everything that links you to Tarnagar. If Sigmundus's soldiers came and searched the city, they might not find you but they might find your old clothes and that would make it easier to track you down.'

Apart from equipping themselves with a new wardrobe, those first days were mostly spent sightseeing. Albigen and Maeve took them for long walks around the city, exploring Moiteera's many faded treasures. They showed them the city's art gallery, full of portraits of famous citizens whose deeds had long been forgotten. They visited magnificent banqueting halls where those same citizens had celebrated their wealth, a gloomy looking prison where criminals had been locked up, and the city's museum where, among other extraordinary sights, they saw a model of a flying machine.

Albigen informed them that Sigmundus had once possessed hundreds of the aeroplanes until the Púca destroyed his entire fleet.

'It was the first action in which I took part,' he told them, enthusiastically. 'Up until that time the Púca had concentrated on trying to halt the production of Ichor. But Sigmundus was aware that we had made our base in the ruined city and it was only a matter of time before he sent his airforce against us. So we decided to strike first. Sigmundus was careless in those days and he kept his whole fleet together in one place, a military base a hundred miles to the north of here. It took us three days to get there and we arrived at nightfall. It wasn't difficult to carry out our mission. There were four hundred and fifty planes and we laid explosives beneath every single one. After we'd finished there was nothing but wreckage.'

'But can't he just build them again?'

'Of course he can. He's trying to, even as we speak. But progress is slow. That's one of the side effects of Ichor that he didn't bargain for. The minds of those who take it become timid and petty, not daring to suggest anything original or unusual in case it might put their careers at risk. They have difficulty retainingknowledge and they lose the ability to make decisions, innovate or improvise. The society that Sigmundus has built is aging before its time. And of course none of the neighbouring countries will come to its aid.'

Both Dante and Bea looked confused at this.

'What do you mean?' Bea asked. 'How could the barbarians be of any help to Sigmundus?'

Albigen grinned widely. 'Haven't you worked that out yet?' he asked. 'All those tales they tell you at school about how the rest of the world sank into lawlessness and barbarism are just a pack of lies. Our neighbours get on very well without Ichor. We are the barbarians, not them.'

'How can you say that?' Bea demanded, angrily.

'Because it's true. You can't imagine how differently they live. Their citizens are free. If they wish to criticise their leaders, they do so. Unfortunately they don't want anything to do with us. They consider us a diseased country.'

Bea stared at him in disbelief but Dante was less sceptical. He had never known much about the rest of the world in the first place and he was quite prepared to accept the possibility that everything he had been told was a lie.

He was more preoccupied with the enormous machine that stood in the middle of the gallery like a great steel bird. The more he gazed at it, the more certain he felt that sooner or later Sigmundus would manage to rebuild his fleet, with or without help from outside. And when he did so neither Moiteera nor anywhere else would offer them a refuge.

For Dante the most memorable visit of all was to the lofty towers of the old university in the west of the city. The lecture halls were empty now and the sound of his footsteps echoed eerily as he walked between the rows of wooden desks where once students had sat and listened to learned professors discourse on every subject under the sun. But the library was still full of ancient books and it was here, Maeve told him, that his mother had spent her time when she was exiled, and it was here, too, that his parents had met.

Dante could not read any of the books but he took them down from the shelves, feeling the weight of them in his hands and marvelling at all the learning they contained. While the others wandered off to explore the laboratories, he stayed behind, sitting in one of the leather-backed chairs, watching dust motes swirling about in the sunbeams that poured through the great arched windows. After a while it seemed to him that he could almost see his mother's shadowy form seated in a corner of the room, bent over one of the ancient books, searching for the knowledge and power that would enable her to fight back against Sigmundus.

After he had been in Moiteera for a week, Dante was sitting in the courtyard of the hotel when Albigen arrived, looking very serious.

'Ezekiel wants to see you,' he said. 'He's waiting at the top of the Tower of State.'

Built hundreds of years earlier as a symbol of the city's independence, the Tower of State stood not far from the hotel. It was at the top of this great monument that Ezekiel chose to spend much of his time, gazing out over Moiteera and making his plans.

Dante went through the thick wooden door at the base of the building and began the slow climb up the winding stairs. He counted four hundred and twenty before finally stepping out onto the platform at the top, his legs almost too weak to hold him upright.

Ezekiel was leaning against the railing, looking down on the city. He turned to greet Dante. 'It's a long climb,' he observed.

Dante went and stood beside him, too out of breath to answer. The view from the tower both fascinated and horrified him, reminding him vividly of his mother's death and of his own nightmares. He stared down at the city, spread out beneath him like a picture in one of the books he had glimpsed in the university library, until, seized by dizziness, he stepped back from the edge.

'Every brick in this tower was laid by hand,' Ezekiel told him. 'Just think of the work that must have involved. And yet the task we face is vastly more difficult.'

'What task is that?' Dante asked.

Ezekiel smiled grimly. 'The defeat of our enemy, of course. Why else do you think I brought you here?'

'But is that really possible?' Dante asked. 'I mean how many Púca are there? A hundred? A hundred and fifty?'

'One hundred and thirty-seven, including children. And we face an army of thousands, a security force that is just as large, an obedient public and the entire medical establishment. Yet things are not as hopeless as they seem. Sigmundus has created a society of hollow people. Their spirits are weak from years of taking Ichor. Soldiers lack aggression, and their officers shy away from using their initiative or taking risks. What is more, people are losing their technological skills. When machines go wrong, it gets harder and harder to find anyone who can fix them. The country is on the brink of ruin even more surely than this city. It merely looks secure from the outside.'

'So why don't we just wait for it to crumble?' Dante asked.

'Because it is our country,' Ezekiel replied fiercely. 'Just because Sigmundus stole it from us, doesn't mean we should stand back and let it be destroyed.'

'Then what can we do about it?'

'As you have pointed out, it is not realistic to imagine we might defeat our enemy through conventional means. But there is another way.'

'What's that?'

'You saw it in action on Tarnagar.'

'You mean when the world seemed to stop?'

'Exactly.'

'You still haven't explained how you did that.'

Ezekiel nodded. 'That is why I have brought you here today. But first let us sit down.'

They went and sat with their backs to the entrance to the stairs and Ezekiel resumed his explanation. 'It was Yashar who first taught me how to do it. After she was exiled here, she was determined to fight back but without the resources at her disposal, it wasn't easy. However, she always insisted that the first and most important tool of any researcher is the mind. So she spent her days thinking about everything she had learned during her time at the institute. Some of her simpler experiments, such as the Dragon's Teeth, she was able to duplicate. And we have made use of them to defend ourselves. But to Yashar these were no more than tricks. She was determined to manipulate Odyllic Force without the aid of technology, simply by using the power of the mind.'

'You mean – just by thinking about it?'

'There is a great deal more involved than merely thinking about it,' Ezekiel replied, 'but in essence you are correct. Let me show you something.' Getting to his feet, he walked over to the barrier which ran round the perimeter of the platform.

Dante stood up, too. 'What are you going to do?' he asked, seized by a sense of foreboding.

'Watch,' Ezekiel told him.

The barrier was about chest height, made of wire mesh with a guard rail running along the top. Ezekiel put his hands on the top and began clambering over. A moment later he was balanced precariously on the other side, still facing Dante but with his back to a sheer drop. He glanced over his shoulder, then turned back to look at Dante.

'It's a long way down, isn't it?' he said. 'If I were to fall, my body would be utterly smashed on the paving stones below.'

'Stop it!' Dante hissed. 'Whatever you're trying to prove, this isn't the way to do it.'

'Isn't it?' Ezekiel asked. He raised one eyebrow and then, without warning, let go of the rail.

Dante opened his mouth to scream but no sound came out. He staggered over to the barrier and peered frantically over the edge.

'Looking for someone?' Ezekiel asked. He was standing behind Dante.

'How did you do that?' Dante demanded in astonishment.

'Everything that can possibly happen always does,' Ezekiel told him, 'but some of those possibilities we choose to believe in. Those are the ones we call reality. By manipulating Odyllic Force I changed the pattern of that reality.' He clambered back over the rail again.

'Why did you make me watch that?' Dante asked. His astonishment was gradually being replaced by anger.

'Because you will never succeed until you have faced your worst nightmares.'

'Then perhaps I don't want to succeed!'

'That is your choice, of course. But I think your mother and father would be disappointed.'

It was impossible to argue with such a statement. Instead, Dante stood in silence for a long time trying to understand what he had just witnessed. Finally, he spoke.

'All right then,' he said, his voice still full of anger, 'but tell me this: if you are so powerful, why don't you just walk right up to Sigmundus and kill him? After all, he couldn't stop you.'

'If only it were that simple,' Ezekiel replied. 'Unfortunately Sigmundus is already dead. That is the real problem.'

THE PARLIAMENT OF BIRDS

Dante stared at him in astonishment. 'But that's ridiculous!' he said.

'Is it any more ridiculous than jumping off a building and not hitting the ground?'

'But he can't be dead.'

'Why not?'

'Because...because everybody would know.'

'Not everybody, just some people. You needn't look at me like that. It's true, I promise you. Sigmundus has been dead for years.'

'What do you mean?'

'I'm not sure I can explain it to you at this time.'

'At least try!'

But infuriatingly, Ezekiel shook his head. 'Sigmundus is dead. That's all you need to know for now. When you've got a little further with your training, you might be able to understand.'

'What training?'

'Your training as a Púca warrior, of course.'

'Who said I wanted to be a warrior?' This conversation was moving so fast it was bewildering Dante.

'You declared as much when you walked out of the

main gate back on Tarnagar,' Ezekiel told him. 'How else do you imagine you are going to survive? Starting tomorrow, you and Bea will join the classes in fighting run by Manachee in the old school near the Boulevard of Lovers. In the evenings I will be teaching you about Odyllic Force. And, of course, you will have to learn to read and write.'

Dante looked dismayed. 'It's too late for reading and writing,' he said. 'I should have learned that when I was little.'

'That's very true,' Ezekiel replied. 'But now you have a chance to catch up on what you missed.'

Nothing Dante could say would dissuade him. 'Your father was a great man of letters,' he insisted. 'Don't you want to read his poetry one day?'

Reluctantly, Dante agreed.

'One last thing,' Ezekiel said. 'What I told you about Sigmundus is for your ears only. The others are not ready to hear it. Do you understand?'

Dante nodded uncertainly.

'Good. Then our conversation is over.' Ezekiel returned to gazing thoughtfully out over the city and there was nothing left for Dante but to make his way back down the winding stairs to the street below.

As he stepped out onto the street, he saw Perdita standing on the other side of the road peering at him. He would have ignored her but she crossed the road to speak to him.

'So you've been summoned to the tower, have you?' she began.

'I don't know what you mean by summoned,' Dante said. 'I've been talking to Ezekiel, that's all.'

'Getting your instructions, more like,' Perdita said, scornfully. 'I suppose he's started training you?'

'I don't see that it's any business of yours.'

Perdita looked unperturbed by his response. 'Perhaps it is and perhaps it isn't, but I bet he hasn't told you everything, has he?' She waited for him to respond and when he remained silent, she nodded. 'I suppose he said that's because you wouldn't understand? I can see by your face that I'm close to the mark. Well I'll let you in on a secret. Ezekiel wants you to learn to use Odyllic Force, doesn't he? But he hasn't explained that there are things out there waiting for you.'

'What sort of things?'

'I don't know what they are, exactly,' Perdita admitted. 'But what do you think made my Eugenius the way he is today?' She stared at him, her eyes lit up with a manic intensity.

'I've no idea.'

'Eugenius wanted to manipulate Odyllic Force too. He wanted to be like your precious mother and like Ezekiel – someone who could take hold of the fabric of this world and twist it to suit himself. But something got hold of him first. And it sucked the life out of him, left him a mere shell. How long do you think he's been like that? Go on, guess.'

Dante shook his head, intimidated by the fury in her voice.

'Sixteen years,' she went on, bitterly. 'Sixteen long

214

years. In all that time he hasn't spoken a word. He just goes on from day to day, not even aware that he exists. And the same thing could happen to you. So I'd think twice before following Ezekiel's orders.'

With that, she turned and strode off down the road, her black shawl fluttering in the wind.

Lessons started the very next day in an old school building not far from the hotel. Dante soon discovered that they were not as bad as he had expected. The atmosphere was relaxed and the teachers were friendly. Students were encouraged to ask questions as well as to answer them. Nevertheless, to his humiliation, he found he had to share some of his classes with much younger children. While most of the other pupils already knew a great deal, he had to start from the very beginning, learning the letters of the alphabet. His teacher was Keeva, Maeve's mother. She was kind and patient but she would not allow him to give up, although he wanted to at first.

Over the next couple of weeks, Dante made painful progress. Sometimes he felt like stamping his foot in frustration as he struggled to cope with information that children half his age found simple. Then Keeva would remind him calmly, but firmly, that it was impossible to defeat your enemy if you could not first win a battle with yourself.

He found the afternoons much more to his liking. Here the focus was on learning to fight, and it was easy enough to see how these skills would be crucial. Everyone took part, whatever their age, and Dante soon discovered that he could pick up what was being taught a lot more readily than some of his more experienced fellow students. He began to enjoy the afternoons almost as much as he disliked the mornings.

But Bea was not finding it quite so easy to learn to fight. Her muscles ached from the exercises she was given to build up her strength, and she found it galling that someone like Maeve, who was so slight to look at, could pin her to the ground with the greatest of ease.

'I just don't see the point of all this,' she complained one day. Maeve had been explaining how a particular move involved using the enemy's strength to defeat them, rather than using your own strength. 'Why do we need to learn to fight at all? Surely, if the troops turn up, one of the Púca can use Odyllic Force to stop them.'

Maeve smiled. 'I'm afraid it's not so easy,' she said. 'Ezekiel is the only one who can do that.'

'I thought Yashar had shown everyone how to do it.'

'Everyone here has tried and we continue to do so. But no one except Yashar and Ezekiel have ever succeeded. That's why Ezekiel has such high hopes for Dante, and why he allowed himself to be captured, in the hope of rescuing him. Many of us were against the plan. They pointed out that Yashar had not come back from Tarnagar and they believed the same thing might happen to Ezekiel.'

'They underestimated him, then,' Bea said.

'Perhaps. But it was a terrible risk. We might have

216

lost our leader and our greatest weapon at the same time. That's why we can't just rely on Ezekiel's skill. The troops are sent to attack us regularly. We've placed Dragon's Teeth all around the city, but sometimes the soldiers get past them and we're forced to defend ourselves. And then there are the actions, when we try to disrupt the distribution of Ichor, or when we hear about another "misfit" who needs to be rescued.'

'Like me?' Bea asked. She wasn't sure she liked to hear herself described as a 'misfit'.

'Like all of us,' Maeve reassured her. 'We're all misfits, and proud of it. Now, shall we start training again?'

A few days later Albigen asked Dante and Bea if they were ready to join the special lessons that Ezekiel held in the school in the evenings. It was what Dante had been hoping to hear, but also what he most feared. He knew that the Púca expected great things of him because he was Yashar's son, and he badly wanted to live up to their expectations. But what if that was impossible? What if he were no better than anyone else? And although he had not discussed it with anyone, he worried, too, about Perdita's warning. Almost every day since their confrontation at the base of the tower, he had watched as she led Eugenius into the dining room. She said nothing further to Dante but her obvious misery and the dreadful fate of her son was like a bloodstain on a white wall, something that could not be ignored, no matter how hard you tried.

That evening Dante and Bea turned up at the appointed time. The inside of the school hall had been lit by candles that threw flickering shadows on the walls and filled the air with the fragrance of burning wax, a smell that Bea was beginning to associate with life in Moiteera. Rugs had been spread on the floor and Ezekiel's audience sat cross-legged in the middle of the room. Among the students, there were a few older Púca but the majority of the audience was made up of young people.

'Those of you who have come to this class before will already have heard what I am going to tell you,' Ezekiel began. 'Those of you who have come for the first time will soon become familiar with it. What I have to say is not new, but the meaning will only become clear when you put it into practice. Look around you. This is an ancient and substantial building. A great deal of thought and hard work went into the making of it.' He knocked on the ground with his knuckles. 'The floor and the walls are solid enough but I promise you, this is all an illusion.'

Bea frowned. How could the very building in which they were sitting be an illusion?

'Beneath this everyday world,' Ezekiel continued, 'runs the energy of the Odyll, like an underground river that is always flowing. The path to gaining control of that energy lies in our dreams.'

It was still a little shocking for Bea to hear someone talk in public about dreams and she glanced round the room to see how other people were reacting. No one else seemed to find it disturbing.

'Dreams are the cauldrons of your desires,' Ezekiel went on. 'They are the places where hopes are born and where your hidden fears rise up to confront you. But the ability to control your dreams is within your grasp. And once you learn to take hold of that ability, it is only a matter of time before you begin to see the lines of force all around you. Then you finally understand that anything is possible for those who possess the courage to impose their will upon the world of the Odyll. But that comes later. First we must learn to draw power to ourselves. So let us start by learning to focus our minds on the task that awaits us.'

He began to describe a series of exercises designed to increase their powers of concentration. First, he placed a candle on the floor in front of him and asked them to stare at it.

'Let your mind become the candle flame,' he told them, 'and let the rest of the world retreat into the shadows. Do not try to forget about the world – that is only another way of noticing it. Just accept it while you continue to focus on the candle flame.'

Bea did as she was instructed, staring at the little yellow tongue of flame until her vision blurred. She was just beginning to drift off to sleep when Ezekiel began to speak again.

'Now I want you to hold your hands out in front of you, palms facing upwards. Focus on your hands. Try to fix in your mind exactly what they look like so that you could recognise them even if you didn't know they were your own.'

Bea almost laughed out loud when he said this. How could someone not know they were looking at their own hands?

'When someone finally succeeds in coming awake in their dreams for the first time,' Ezekiel continued, 'the shock is so great they invariably wake up again immediately, and everything they have been striving for is lost. So it is important to have something to focus on, something that will keep you in the world of your dreams even though your mind has regained its alertness. If you have trained yourself to focus on your hands in the waking world, you can do so in the dream world. The sight of your hands becomes an anchor while you adjust to your new surroundings.'

For at least an hour, he continued to outline exercises intended to develop their powers of visualisation and concentration. None of them worked for Bea. Finally, to her relief, he decided they'd had enough for the evening.

'You must never give up hope,' he told them before allowing them to leave. 'It may take years to achieve success.'

But it was clear, afterwards, that some of the others had already given up hope. 'I'll never learn,' Albigen admitted to Dante, as they walked back to the hotel together.

'Then why do you still go to the classes?'

'To encourage the others, I suppose. If they saw me give up, they might do the same.'

This was probably true, since many of the younger

Púca looked up to Albigen. He was their most skilful fighter and Ezekiel had put him in charge of one of the patrols that regularly reconnoitred the city on the lookout for soldiers.

'Doesn't it depress you, going along to the classes without any hope of ever succeeding?' Dante asked.

Albigen shook his head. 'I may have given up hope for myself,' he said, 'but I'm sure someone's going to succeed one of these days and I think I know who it's going to be.' He winked at Dante and gave him one of his lopsided grins.

At weekends there were no lessons. Many of the older Púca disappeared to tend the fruit and vegetable gardens they cultivated in different parts of the city. The younger ones relaxed, letting off steam by playing football and other sports, practising their strange, meandering music, or just hanging around gossiping. Dante usually spent his spare time with Albigen, but on the third weekend after his arrival, Albigen's patrol was on duty, scouting around the northern suburbs, so Dante was left to his own devices.

He decided to pay a visit to the Parliament of Birds. Albigen had told him about it a few days earlier. It was a green wilderness to the north of the city. Once it had been a magnificent public park but when the population of Moiteera was wiped out, there was no one left to look after it. In a remarkably short space of time, nature had begun to reclaim its own. Now, the park was

221

completely overgrown, a jungle of trees and bushes that had become a nesting place for thousands of the city's birds.

'You can hear them from over a mile away,' Albigen had told him. 'It sounds as though they're holding a great conference. That's why we call it the Parliament of Birds. You should go there when the sun's setting and the birds have all come home to roost. It's the sound of the world before mankind set foot on it.'

Dante decided to call on Bea first, to see whether she wanted to come with him. He had not seen much of her recently. There had been so many new people to meet and so much to learn that, although their paths crossed often enough, they hardly ever spent any time alone.

When he knocked on her door, there was no answer and he thought at first that she must have gone out. He was just turning away when the door opened and Bea peered out. 'Oh hello, Dante,' she said.

She sounded miserable and he could tell from her eyes that she'd been crying. 'What's the matter?' he asked. 'Are you ill?'

'No, I'm fine.'

'You don't look fine.'

'I've just been feeling sorry for myself, that's all. Do you want to come in?'

'Thanks.'

She led the way into her room and sat down on the bed. Dante sat in a leather armchair by the window and studied her tear-stained face. 'So what's the matter?' he asked. 'Has someone said something to upset you?'

Bea shook her head. 'No. Everyone's been really nice to me. It's just that...' She hesitated. 'It sounds so stupid!'

'Why don't you let me be the judge of that?'

She sighed. 'All right. It's just that I've been feeling a bit homesick.'

'Homesick!' Dante could hardly believe his ears.

'I said you'd think it was stupid.'

'I didn't say it was stupid,' he objected. 'I'm just surprised, that's all.'

'I can see it wouldn't make any sense to you,' she told him, 'but I miss my parents. I know I didn't get on with them, but they were still my mum and dad.'

'I'm sorry, that must be hard.'

'I don't mean I want to go back or anything. But some days I really feel it. Like today – because it's my birthday.'

Dante looked at her with dismay. 'I'm sorry, I didn't know.'

'Of course you didn't. And I'd rather you didn't tell anyone else. It's just that if I was at home today, everyone would be making a big fuss over me.'

'They'd also be giving you Ichor.'

'Yes, but at least I'd be somebody special, whereas here I'm nobody.'

'You wouldn't have been somebody special for very long. If the Ichor had worked you'd have become like all the others, too scared to break the rules, having to content yourself with looking down on anyone less important than yourself and being pushed around by those of a higher rank. If it hadn't worked, you'd have been like me – a freak.'

'You're not a freak.'

'I was on Tarnagar.'

'I suppose so. All the same, I sometimes wonder what I'm doing here. It's different for you. You're Yashar Cazabon's son. You belong here. But I'm just someone who got swept up in the process of rescuing you.'

Dante considered telling her about his fear that he would not fulfil the hopes the Púca had pinned on him, that he would never learn to use Odyllic Force. But he decided to keep this to himself for now.

'Most of the people here have got a story like yours,' he said. 'OK, there are a few, like Maeve, who were born into the Púca, but the majority of them just found their way here without meaning to, simply because there was no other place for them to go. Besides, what about your dreams?'

'What about them?'

'Don't you think they're proof that you belong here? That's what Ezekiel thought, isn't it? And everyone respects his opinion.'

'I know,' Bea said. 'I suppose I'm just being childish. You won't tell anyone about this, will you?'

'Of course not.'

'Promise?'

'I promise.'

'Thanks.'

He tried to persuade her to come with him to the Parliament of Birds but she preferred to stay in her room. 'Don't worry about me,' she told him. 'I feel better now that I've talked to someone about it.'

'Are you sure?'

'I'm certain. I'll go and find Maeve. She's helping her mum and dad with their vegetable garden. You go and listen to the birds. I expect they'll talk more sense than me.'

She had cheered up considerably by this time, so Dante felt happier about leaving her on her own. He made his way out of the hotel and followed the directions Albigen had given him.

The sound of birdsong grew louder and louder as he approached the park, as if every kind of bird in existence had decided to send a representative to the park to make its views known. Two huge iron gates stood open at the entrance and he followed the tarmac path that led inside. It was cracked and pitted and plants had pushed their way through the fissures. The grass on either side of the path had grown wild and coarse. Thistles, nettles and brambles had run riot in the flowerbeds. The trees, once carefully pruned and pollarded, had been left at liberty to spread their branches and there the birds sat, in their thousands, loudly declaring their presence.

The air in here smelled different from outside, more earthy. It was the odour of growth and decay, a fragrance that vividly brought back the woods on Tarnagar. This, in turn, reminded him of the little collection of carvings he had left behind on the windowsill of his attic room. It was the only thing he regretted about the hastiness of his departure. He decided he would carve something new, and began to look around for a suitable piece of wood.

As he rounded a bend, his way was blocked by an enormous tree that had fallen across the path. The force of its fall had torn the roots out of the ground and they stretched out into the air like gnarled fingers, vainly seeking to clutch at some support. He sat down on the trunk and listened to the birds for a long time. While he did so, he wondered about what Ezekiel had told him. Could Sigmundus really be dead? And if so, why did everyone act as if he was still alive? The more he thought about it, the less sense it made.

After a while he got up and wandered on a little further. Someone had come along earlier with a saw and cut away some of the branches of the fallen tree and a little pile of logs had been heaped up at the side of the path. When Dante noticed these he bent down and turned them over one by one, assessing their suitability for carving. They were still sound enough. Finally, he found one that he liked the look of, tucked it under his arm and set off back home.

When he returned, he found a fire burning in the street outside the hotel. Food was being barbecued, the musicians had started to play and another impromptu party was in swing. He looked around for Bea and found her, along with Maeve, getting potatoes ready to roast in the embers of the fire.

'What was the Parliament of Birds like?' she asked.

'Noisy and wild.'

'A bit like the Púca then,' Maeve said.

It was tempting to stay and join the party, but after having something to eat, Dante decided to retire for the night. While he had been walking back from the park he had decided what he wanted to carve, and he was keen to make a start. As soon as he had shut the door of his room, he sat down with his back against the bed. Using a knife Manachee had given him when he had first started learning to fight, he began stripping away the bark and the outer wood from the log. He cut out the shape very roughly at first. It would take him hours to complete, he knew that, but he did not mind. He did not feel the least bit sleepy. Instead, he was completely taken over by the excitement of creating something beautiful from the raw wood, and he continued to work steadily through the hours of darkness until the stars had disappeared from the little patch of sky he could see through his window and the morning sun had risen once more.

His body was stiff from hunching over the carving and his fingers ached. There was a pile of wood shavings on the floor but in his hand he held the shape of a bird. He inspected it from every angle and decided he was satisfied with it. Now, at last, he could get some rest. Taking off his clothes, he fell into bed, utterly exhausted. Sleep came almost immediately.

It was midday before he woke. Yawning, he sat up in bed. Then he remembered the carving. He dressed quickly and went downstairs to the floor below, where Bea had her room. He knocked on the door, and a moment later she opened it.

'Oh hello,' she said. 'What happened to you last night? You disappeared really early.'

'I had something to do,' he told her. He held out his hand to show her the bird. 'It's a birthday present,' he said. 'I'm sorry it's late.'

She took the bird from him and inspected it. 'Oh Dante, it's lovely,' she said. 'Did you really make it for me?'

'Yes.'

'That's the nicest thing anyone's ever done for me.' She leaned forward and, to his great surprise, she kissed him on the lips. 'Thank you,' she said. 'I'll never forget this, as long as I live.'

THE ATTACK

Everyone agreed that it was the most beautiful spring Moiteera had known since the Púca's arrival. The blossoms stayed on the trees in the Boulevard of Lovers for weeks and even Bea forgot her homesickness and began finding her feet.

The change began during one of the afternoon fighting sessions. Manachee was explaining how to defend yourself against an attack from behind, and Bea and Maeve were practising together. In theory, Bea knew what she was supposed to do, but making her body do it at fighting speed was another matter.

'It's no use,' she said, dejectedly. 'I'm never going to be any good at this.'

'Perhaps I could help,' Albigen suggested. He and Dante usually worked together but it was common for people to swap partners.

'There's something wrong with me,' Bea told him. 'I can't get my body to co-operate.' Nevertheless, she agreed to let Albigen help her.

He was a good teacher, gently pointing out the mistakes she'd been making and praising her when she got the moves right. 'You have to let your body learn by itself,' he told her. 'Stop thinking about it and let your instinct take over.'

By the end of the session, she had finally begun to trust her own sense of balance. Instead of snatching clumsily at her opponent, she was starting to use his own momentum to defeat him. When the session was over she had a big smile on her face.

'That was the first time I've ever enjoyed fighting,' she told him.

From that day onwards, Bea regularly trained with Albigen. Dante watched this with mixed feelings. He liked Albigen – it was hard not to like him – and he was happy that Bea was feeling more at home with the Púca, but deep inside him, something rankled. It was as if the more Bea took from Albigen, the less Dante could give her. He knew this feeling was not something to be proud of and he kept quiet about it, trying to pretend – even to himself – that it didn't exist.

He began redoubling his efforts to control Odyllic Force. Every evening he turned up for Ezekiel's special lessons, and practised focusing his will so that it was as finely honed as the point of a knife. Every night before he surrendered to sleep, he went through the rituals that Ezekiel had described, telling himself that this would be the night when he came awake in his dreams. As he descended slowly towards unconsciousness, he concentrated on his breathing, imagining that with each breath outwards, he was expelling from his mind all the distractions of the day, all the minor irritations and fears that might prevent him succeeding. He breathed in slowly, imagining his body filling up with energy and power. He told himself that he was ready for the experience, that he wanted it more than anything else in the world, and he slipped gently into the velvet tunnel of sleep believing in his heart that this night would be the turning point. Yet each morning he woke with the same bitter sense of disappointment.

Finally, he decided to talk to Ezekiel about it directly. He sought him out at the top of the Tower of State and raised the subject of his lack of progress.

Ezekiel seemed unsurprised. 'You have only just set out on the journey,' he replied. 'You cannot possibly expect to see results so soon.'

'But I don't feel any different,' Dante pointed out. 'After every training session I expect to feel something has changed inside me, but nothing ever happens.'

'You are worrying unnecessarily. When you're ready, I have no doubt you will succeed.'

'Yes but what if I'm never ready?'

'You will be. When you've learned to let go.'

Dante found this answer typical of Ezekiel – hinting at things but refusing to explain them clearly. 'What do I have to learn to let go of?' he demanded.

'Your fear and your pride,' Ezekiel told him.

Dante found this hard to accept. After years spent taking orders from absolutely everyone, he was a person of some importance for the first time in his life. It was hard not to feel proud – and also a little frightened that he would never live up to the expectations of others.

'You will never be able to enter the path of dreams while you still treasure the feelings and attachments of this world,' Ezekiel insisted. 'Let me tell you something. Your mother was much more powerful than I am, but Sigmundus was able to capture her and imprison her in the asylum. Why do you think that happened?'

'I don't know,.'

'It was because of you.'

'Because of me?' Dante stared back at him.

'Yes. Once you were born, your mother's love for you bound her to this world. When she came face to face with Sigmundus, her powers deserted her. She was just an ordinary human being. And that is what you will be, as long as you continue to focus on the world around you. You must forget yourself, Dante. Think only of the path that stretches before you, the way of power. That is how you become a master of Odyllic Force.'

Afterwards, Dante walked through the streets for a long time, thinking about what Ezekiel had said until he found himself in the square where the statue of his father was. He stood gazing up at the poet's enigmatic smile and wondering what Alvar Kazimir Mendini had really been like. Had he been the kind of person who spoke out bravely no matter who tried to silence him? Or had he been a reluctant hero?

He turned sadly away from the statue. What he really wanted, he decided, was to be just another member of the Púca, not a leader or the son of a leader but an ordinary individual. A footsoldier. He was ready to do his bit when he was called upon, as long as it was something he was sure he could do. The others were always talking about the actions they had participated in – how dangerous and how exciting they were – and Dante had been waiting eagerly for the chance to make his own contribution.

By the time he had made his way back to the hotel, lunch was being served. He had just sat down with some of the other younger Púca when Bea walked in, grinning all over her face.

'You're looking very pleased with yourself,' he observed.

'I've just been told that I'm joining Albigen's patrol,' she told him.

'Congratulations,' Dante said, trying to sound sincere. Mechanically, he finished his food, then got to his feet and left the room without another word.

It was Manachee's policy to insist on his students swapping partners from time to time. So it came as no surprise when Dante and Bea found themselves facing each other during the following day's training session. They were practising a new combination of attacking and defensive moves.

'You can use the moves in any order,' Manachee told them, 'but the secret is to create one set of expectations in your enemy's mind and then surprise them by doing something completely different.'

The last time they had fought, Bea had been so clumsy and slow that Dante could easily tell what she was trying to do in advance. This time, however, she stood in front of him, swaying gently from side to side and he was unsure from which direction she was going to attack. Suddenly her right arm snaked out and seized his left arm. At the same time her left leg locked itself around his right leg and he found himself tumbling to the ground. He tried to roll away but she still had hold of his arm which she was bending up behind his back. Furiously, he kicked out with his legs and he felt her grip loosen. He used all his strength to twist out of the hold and was back on his feet again.

'Not bad,' he said, 'but you won't be so lucky next time.'

'Luck had nothing to do with it,' she calmly assured him.

Dante opened his mouth to reply but before he could say another word, Bea leaped towards him, feet first. At the last minute she seemed to swivel in the air and her right foot shot out, catching him in the ribs. Shocked and winded, he went flailing backwards. In an instant, Bea had regained her balance and thrown herself on top of him. Now she held him in a neck-lock from which he could not break free, no matter how hard he struggled.

'Surrender?' she demanded, gleefully.

'All right, all right.'

She released him from the hold and Dante stood up, angrily dusting himself down. 'That kick wasn't in the sequence we were supposed to be practising,' he pointed out.

'Yes, but you have to be ready for anything,' she

replied. 'It's all about surprise, remember.'

'Surprise isn't the same thing as cheating.'

Bea frowned. 'This isn't a game, Dante,' she told him, solemnly. 'When you're out on patrol, it may be a matter of life and death.' She was so pleased with her success, it never occurred to her that these words might be painful for Dante.

He flushed bright red. 'You think you're so clever, just because you've joined Albigen's patrol, but we all know why that happened, don't we?' He knew he sounded petty and mean, but at that moment he didn't care.

Bea looked shocked. 'I don't know what you're talking about.'

'Don't you?'

'No, I don't.'

Dante raised one eyebrow. 'Come off it, Bea.'

Bea stared back at him without saying anything but her lower lip began to tremble. 'She's going to cry,' Dante thought to himself and the thought brought a distinct thrill of triumph with it.

Bea turned and walked out of the room and Maeve immediately ran after her. It was only then Dante realised that everyone in the room was staring at him.

The lesson had already been running late. Now Manachee hurriedly dismissed them and, afterwards, Dante hurried outside to look for Bea.

Albigen came over to speak to him. 'Just for the record,' he said, his jaw clenched with anger, 'it wasn't my decision to ask Bea to join the patrol. It was Ezekiel's.'

Dante could tell from the tone of Albigen's voice that it was true. 'Sorry,' he said.

'I'm not the one you should be apologising to.'

It wasn't fair, Dante thought, as he made his way miserably back to his room in the hotel. Bea had cheated, however much she tried to justify it. He closed the door of his room, lay on the bed and closed his eyes. He would have liked to block the world out completely, to fall asleep and forget about his problems but it was too early in the day. Instead, he listened idly to the sounds outside his window and wished he had kept his feelings to himself.

He decided not to bother with dinner that evening. By now the others would all have heard about his argument with Bea and the idea of going downstairs and facing their accusing looks was not appealing. Instead, he watched through his window as evening set in over Moiteera. The sunsets had been extraordinarily beautiful for the last few weeks and today's was no exception. The sky had just begun to change from a blazing red to a deep violet when he heard a series of very loud bangs that made him jump to his feet and run to the window. He could see nothing outside and, at first, he could think of no explanation for what he had heard. Then, suddenly, it dawned on him: the sound was gunfire!

More shots broke out as he turned and ran downstairs. A lot of Púca had already assembled in the Mendini Room. Some of them were carrying guns and boxes of ammunition.

Maeve came up to him. 'I was just going to look for you,' she said. 'Ezekiel was here a moment ago and he asked me to make sure you were safe.'

'Where's he gone now?'

'To see what he can do to help.'

'Where are the enemy?'

'In the north of the city. They must have got through the Dragon's Teeth somehow and encountered Albigen's patrol.'

'What should we do?'

'Wait. That's all we can do. If Ezekiel wants us to do anything else, he'll get word to us.'

'But we can't just sit here!'

Maeve sighed. 'I know it isn't easy but it's best to stay calm and to try to be patient. They may not stay very long. They don't like getting bogged down in hand-to-hand fighting. This may be just a show of force.'

Her attempts at reassurance did not convince Dante. Now that the troops had finally made their move, he felt certain they would not just turn around and go home as soon as they met a bit of resistance. By now, most of the armed Púca had left to take up defensive positions. Dante hated having to hide in the basement like a child, but Ezekiel's orders had been very clear.

After a while Manachee appeared in the entrance. His usually amiable face looked grim.

'What's happening?' Maeve asked.

'There are more troops than we expected. Their leaders are forcing them past the Dragon's Teeth.

We're keeping them busy but it isn't easy.'

'I wish I could help,' Dante said.

Manachee shook his head. 'You've got to stay here.'

'Why hasn't Ezekiel stopped them?' Dante asked.

'He can't. He's been wounded. It's all right, it's nothing very serious, just a shrapnel wound, but it's weakened him. Albigen's taken charge of the fighting. He's planning to lead the soldiers into a series of ambushes.'

'Will it work?'

'I think so. They don't know the territory like we do and once they've lost a few men, they'll retreat.'

'How can you be so sure of that?'

'So far they always have. Soldiers who take Ichor find it very hard to be brave – even when they outnumber their opponents.' He gave a forced smile. Then, after a word with Keeva, he disappeared in search of more ammunition.

Time passed slowly. The children lay down on blankets placed on the floor and, one by one, they fell asleep. The adults sat in silence, locked in their own thoughts. Dante was hunched in a corner thinking about Bea, wondering where she was and wishing he had not quarrelled with her.

As the night wore on, the sound of gunfire grew rarer and Púca began drifting back to the hotel in ones and twos. They looked exhausted but they seemed confident. Many of the soldiers had retreated, they told Dante, driven back by a combination of the Dragon's Teeth, booby traps, and sniper fire.

Ezekiel arrived just after midnight with his arm in a sling. He looked weary but grimly determined. 'They're not finding it as easy as they expected,' he assured Dante.

Towards dawn the members of Albigen's patrol began straggling in one by one. Every time a newcomer appeared in the doorway, Dante hoped it would be Bea. At last Albigen himself turned up. 'The soldiers are leaving the city,' he announced.

'Where's Bea?' Dante asked.

Albigen frowned. 'Isn't she here?'

Dante shook his head. 'What's happened to her?'

'I don't know. I told her to make her way back here. She should have arrived by now.'

'Let's not panic,' Ezekiel said. 'She might have got temporarily lost. She doesn't know the city as well as you do. Give her time. She'll turn up.'

Dante sprang to his feet. 'I have to go and look for her,' he said.

Ezekiel shook his head. 'Don't be ridiculous! You haven't got a chance of finding her. She'll come back in her own time. The best thing you can do is go and get some sleep and stop worrying. Bea's a big girl now; she can look after herself.'

At that very moment, however, Bea was sitting inside an abandoned warehouse with her back to the wall and her head raised, listening to soldiers shouting to each other in the street outside. She didn't understand where

239

exactly she had gone wrong but somehow, instead of making her way safely back to the hotel, she had walked straight into an enemy unit. Before she'd had a chance to run, they had seen her and begun firing. Fortunately, their aim was wild and she had managed to duck down an alleyway. Panic-stricken, she had rushed from street to street, taking the first turning that presented itself, never thinking about where she was going, under constant pursuit by the soldiers. Finally, she had found herself in an industrial district and ended up cornered in the warehouse. The soldiers knew more or less where she was, but they were approaching with caution, unaware that Bea had accidentally dropped her rifle while running away.

It had gone eerily silent outside. So Bea decided to risk a glimpse outside. She stood up, her face flattened against the wall and peered out of the window. Immediately she jumped back. They were so much closer than she had feared! There had to be a back exit to the warehouse but it was hard to see anything in this darkness. Trying to make as little noise as possible, she began to creep across the room. But halfway across, there was a splintering sound and the floorboards gave way. Bea screamed as she dropped through space. A split second later she hit the floor below and everything went black.

Dante was standing in the kitchen of the asylum listening to Marsyas telling him that he hadn't washed the dishes properly. Marsyas's face was bright red and his left ear was throbbing.

'The trouble with you,' he told Dante, 'is that your mind is always somewhere else. You seem to think you're too good for this place. All you are is the son of a lunatic who's very lucky not to be locked up himself.'

Dante stared at him in confusion. Surely he hadn't imagined escaping from Tarnagar? Because if he had, then he really must have gone crazy.

Marsyas continued to lecture him about the washing-up, but Dante had stopped listening. He looked round the kitchen and it struck him that there was something very strange about the other workers. Their faces seemed to change whenever he wasn't looking directly at them so that at first it was Jerome who was standing over a chopping board, filleting steak, but then, when he looked again, it was Nathaniel. And now that he came to think about it, it was not just the workers who seemed to be changing: the kitchen itself appeared to shift and transform itself from one moment to the next. He stared at the wall over

Marsyas's left shoulder and it seemed to him that it was swelling and retreating before his eyes, like a living, breathing creature. As he looked more closely, he noticed that the surface of the wall was covered with shapes and patterns that twisted and changed while he watched them.

'This isn't really the asylum kitchen,' he told himself. 'It's like the asylum kitchen but it's somewhere else entirely.'

With this thought came another realisation: he was dreaming! Immediately, an overwhelming sensation of powerlessness began to take hold of him and he felt as though a great wave was heading towards him, one that would wash him back into the waking world. Already its first icy fingers were lapping around his feet as the dream world about him grew fainter. 'You must resist!' he told himself. But how?

Then into his mind came the memory of the exercise Ezekiel had taught him. Immediately, he bowed his head and focused his attention on his hands, forcing himself to notice every line and wrinkle, every subtle gradation of colour. Gradually, the sensation of being swept away subsided. At last he plucked up the courage to raise his eyes and gaze once again at the scene surrounding him. He was still in the kitchen of the asylum, but now Marsyas and the other workers were carrying on with their work as if they could not see him.

Tentatively, Dante took a step forward and discovered that he could walk. With a sense of exhilaration, he made his way across the kitchen towards the back door. Would he be able to manipulate things in this dream world? He stretched out his hand and took hold of the door handle. It felt solid enough beneath his touch. He opened the door and gazed out at the asylum grounds.

There was something exotic about the foliage, as though the very shapes of the leaves held a meaning that was both enticing and menacing. He thought he glimpsed eyes staring back at him from out of the bushes and he half expected wild animals to come bounding across the lawn.

Standing in the doorway, looking out at the scene, he was strongly tempted to explore this world that was so familiar and yet so entirely unknown, but something stopped him. It was a feeling that there was a more important task he needed to do. Something to do with the Púca? As this thought occurred to him, the scene shifted and dissolved and he found himself standing in his room in the hotel in Moiteera, looking down at his body lying on a mattress. It was a very strange sensation and he felt a powerful urge to return to that body. But he was equally sure that he shouldn't do so – not just yet.

He turned his back on his sleeping form and, for a moment, became seized by panic. What if he could not find his way back again? But he breathed deeply and slowly exactly as Ezekiel had shown him and, gradually, he began to feel calmer. He looked around the room. It was as if whenever he wasn't looking directly at something, it unmade itself, dissolving and rearranging its planes and angles to suit the laws of an entirely different geometry. The floor and the ceiling seemed to pulsate with light and strangely familiar symbols flickered across every surface, only to disappear again as he looked more closely. He turned round in a complete circle, like someone who tries to catch an intruder lurking just out of sight. This time he stopped when his circuit was no more than half complete. Where had that small grey door in the wall come from?

He walked slowly towards it and inspected it more closely. The flickering symbols were even stronger here, writhing across the surface like living hieroglyphics. As he watched, they began to swirl round a point in the door, turning faster and faster in concentric circles so that he felt himself being sucked into their centre. Nervously, Dante took a step back and the fierce attraction lessened. He was certain that if he had not used all his willpower to resist, the symbols would have pulled him through into whatever it was that lay beyond the door; but something deep within his being told him that this was not the time, reminding him again that there was an urgent task he had to complete first. He stepped further back, away from the dark gravity of the door. Immediately he remembered his purpose. He needed to discover what had happened to Bea. He sensed that she was in dreadful danger. But how could he find her?

The answer came to him. His dream had begun in the kitchen on Tarnagar, but he had got back to the hotel room simply by thinking about the Púca. So thought alone was enough to take him from place to place – perhaps if he thought hard enough about Bea that would draw him to her? He began to concentrate on bringing her image to mind and immediately he felt the intensity in the room deepen. It was as though an awareness had awakened in the room itself and was regarding him with curiosity, weighing him up and assessing the power of his will. He began to feel as though he was suspended in a great field of energy, a net of power that had a life of its own. He struggled to focus all his thoughts on Bea. For a brief moment the resistance seemed to grow stronger, then he felt it yield and the scene before him began to disintegrate, melting away before his eyes and rearranging itself until he found himself standing in a dark, featureless space. At first he could make out almost nothing, but gradually he became accustomed to the lack of light and his vision began to increase.

He was in the basement of a warehouse near the industrial heart of the city. There were boxes and crates stacked against one wall, but the rest of the place was empty. In a corner of the room a girl was lying on the ground, motionless. He crossed the floor and bent down to look at her more closely. Bea was alive, but only just.

Dante could feel the life inside her like a damaged moth fluttering weakly against a window. There wasn't a second to waste. A flight of stairs brought him to the ground floor and he dashed across the room, skirting the hole where the floor had collapsed. Once he was outside he studied his surroundings, making sure he knew the location of the warehouse. Then he began calling to mind the picture of his own body lying on his bed. Again he felt that sense of deepening intensity and the sensation of being held in the gaze of some vast intelligence. This time, however, there was less resistance. It was as if his right to move about in this dream world had somehow been accepted. Then another shift, and he was back in his hotel room staring down at his inert form on the bed.

He was far from certain of the right way to take repossession of his body and hesitated as he thought about what might happen if he made some dreadful mistake. The memory of Eugenius returned sharply to his mind but he forced it back. Instead, he pictured himself floating on his back just above the bed and almost immediately he found that he was staring up at the ceiling. Satisfied, he closed his eyes and allowed his mind to empty itself completely as he sank gently down into the body beneath him.

He was awake! Jumping out of bed, he ran downstairs. The grey light of dawn was filtering through the high windows of the Mendini Room, revealing a bedraggled collection of figures, some of them sound asleep, others, like Ezekiel, only half awake.

He yawned and stretched his good arm when he saw Dante.

'I know where Bea is!' Dante shouted. He explained how he had come awake in his dream and searched for her.

'Then let's not waste any more time,' Ezekiel replied. 'You must go and bring her back. You'll need a van.

We have several that we keep filled with fuel. Albigen can drive. But be careful. For all we know., there might still be soldiers hanging around.'

'I'll keep my eyes open.'

'One more thing.'

'Yes?'

'Don't build up your hopes too much. The strength of your will has allowed you to find Bea, but she may be beyond our help.'

Dante hoped with all his heart that Ezekiel was wrong. For weeks he had struggled in vain to enter his dreams. To succeed now, only to find he could not bring his friend back from the point of death, would be too awful to bear.

Albigen appeared a few minutes later looking drawn and tired, but when the situation was explained to him, he cast off his weariness. 'Come on,' he said. 'There's a van in one of the garages on the other side of the square.'

As they went out into the street Albigen paused. 'Can you smell burning?' he asked Dante.

'We have to hurry!' Dante urged him, and Albigen nodded, but he looked anxious as he led the way to the garage on the other side of the square.

The van seemed to take ages to start. At last, however, it burst into life, and they raced off in the direction of the industrial district. Fortunately, there was no sign of soldiers, but they had not gone very far before they began to see plumes of black smoke rising into the air.

'They're burning the city!' Albigen exclaimed. He shook his head in dismay. 'I knew our victory was too easy.'

Dante directed him to the warehouse and they parked just outside. It was exactly as Dante had seen it in his dream.

Albigen advanced cautiously towards the hole in the floor and shone his torch down into the space below. 'She's down there all right.'

Carrying a stretcher, they made their way round the edge of the room towards the door in the far corner that opened onto a staircase. At the bottom of the stairs, another door led into the basement. Light filtering through the hole in the floor above, showed where Bea lay on the cold stone floor. They ran over to her and called her name, but she did not respond.

Albigen began to feel for a pulse while Dante waited impatiently. Finally Albigen nodded. 'She's alive, but very weak.'

They eased her gently onto the stretcher, each taking one end and, as gently as they could, brought her up the stairs and back to the van. In the cold light of day her face was deathly white and her skin had a waxy look to it.

'Do you think she's going to make it?' Dante asked when they had stowed her in the back of the van.

'I don't know,' Albigen said. 'Let's see what Ezekiel thinks.'

Neither of them spoke on the journey back.

When they had carried her into the hotel, Ezekiel

lifted one of her eyelids and let it fall again. He spoke her name in her ear but she showed no more sign of responding to his efforts than she had done earlier. Finally, he looked up sadly. 'I'm afraid there's very little we can do for her,' he said.

'What do you mean?' Dante demanded. 'We must be able to do something.'

Ezekiel shook his head. 'She's in a coma.'

'But there must be someone here who can help her, someone with some sort of medical training.'

'Before Sigmundus made me an outlaw, I spent many years studying medicine and working as a doctor,' Ezekiel told him. 'Believe me, we don't have the supplies or the equipment to treat her. As it is, she could die at any time. I'm very sorry, Dante.'

'You can't just give up!' Dante shouted.

'I'm not suggesting we give up,' Ezekiel told him, speaking quietly. 'I'm merely stating the facts. There is one course of action left open to us but it involves terrible risk.'

'What is it?' Dante demanded, eager to snatch at any glimmer of hope.

'Someone must take her to a hospital and leave her in the emergency department.' He looked at Albigen, who nodded gravely.

'But she'll be lost to us,' Dante pointed out. 'As soon as she begins to recover, they'll start giving her Ichor.'

'Whatever happens, she is lost to us,' Ezekiel told him. 'The soldiers are burning the city. We cannot stay here. Those with children are getting ready to leave already. Within the next few hours we will all be gone and we cannot take Bea with us.'

'Where will you go?'

'Forty miles west of here there is a town called Vendas. Ten miles north of Vendas is a wooded area. On the other side of the woods there is a place where people once went to stay for one or two weeks of each year. A holiday village, they called it. The place is abandoned now and completely dilapidated, but it will do for the time being. This is the best we can do for Bea, and the sooner it's done, the better her chances of survival.'

Dante stared miserably at him. He knew that what Ezekiel was saying made sense. Finally, with the heaviest of hearts, he agreed. 'But I'm going with her,' he said, determinedly.

'I don't think that's a good idea.'

'It's my decision.'

Ezekiel nodded. 'If that's what you wish.'

While the others were carrying Bea back to the van, Dante went up to her room. He opened the door and looked around. She had almost no possessions, just a few clothes. He turned to leave but then noticed the wooden bird he had carved for her sitting on the windowsill. He slipped it into his pocket and went back downstairs to where Albigen was waiting for him.

The plan was to make for Bornya, the nearest town large enough to have a hospital. As they drove through the outskirts of Moiteera, the pall of thick black smoke above the city grew denser all the time. At last they joined a wide, empty road heading northwest. It had obviously seen little use for some time – grasses and small plants had pushed their way through the asphalt of the surface.

'Apart from the Púca, nobody goes near Moiteera,' Albigen explained. 'They don't like to be reminded of what happened there.'

After some time they began to encounter other vehicles. At first it was just a few lorries, but gradually the amount of traffic increased until it became a constant flow, and they began to see signs telling them how far it was to Bornya.

As the distances on the signs gradually decreased, Dante replayed in his mind his argument with Bea, and with deep shame he recalled the feeling of triumph he had experienced when he thought she was about to cry. He put his hand in his pocket and felt the bird he had carved for her, remembering the look on her face when he had given it to her and how she had leaned forward and kissed him on the lips. How could he have been so horrible to her?

Soon the green verges on either side of the road began to be replaced by buildings – factories and warehouses at first, then residential areas as they made their way deeper into Bornya. The pedestrians they passed went about their business with bowed heads while the gigantic face of their leader gazed down at them from the sides of buildings.

Before they approached the centre of the city, they turned off the main road, following a sign for the hospital, a huge, grey, featureless building, set by itself in substantial grounds.

Albigen stopped the van outside the emergency entrance, switched off the engine and turned to Dante. 'Are you ready?' he asked.

Dante nodded. 'As ready as I'll ever be.'

They got out of the van and opened the rear doors. Carefully, they lifted Bea out on the stretcher. As they were doing so, Dante noticed a security guard watching them from some distance away. He pointed him out to Albigen.

'Ignore him,' Albigen said. 'Just try and look confident.'

They carried the stretcher in through the main doors. The clinic was full of people sitting in rows of plastic chairs. They regarded the newcomers with curiosity. A receptionist came out from behind her desk, frowning.

'Our friend's had a fall,' Albigen told her. 'She's unconscious.'

The receptionist looked unhappy. 'You should have called an ambulance,' she said.

'Can't you just get a doctor to look at her?'

The receptionist hesitated. 'Take her into treatment room number three,' she said at last.

They carried Bea into the room the receptionist had indicated, setting her down on a trolley just inside the door.

'Now I just need to get some information from you,' she told them.

Albigen shook his head. 'I'm sorry, we can't stop,' he replied.

She looked even more unhappy. 'There's a procedure that must be followed,' she pointed out.

'Please, just get her a doctor right away,' Albigen said. Then he turned and walked out of the room. Dante took the wooden bird out of his pocket and placed it carefully on the stretcher beside Bea. Then he followed Albigen.

'Do you think Bea's going to be all right in there?' Dante asked as they walked briskly through the reception area.

'I hope so,' Albigen replied.

As they came out of the doors, they were stopped in their tracks by the sight of a group of security guards standing around the van.

'Forget the van,' Albigen hissed. 'Just keep walking. Don't look at them.'

They began walking in the opposite direction as quickly as they could without drawing attention to themselves, but it was not long before one of the security guards spotted them.

'Hey, you there!' he shouted.

'Run!' Albigen ordered.

The blood was pounding in Dante's ears and he could hear the sound of footsteps behind him. He glanced over his shoulder and saw, to his dismay, that his pursuers were much closer than he had expected.

The path they were following came out in a yard where ambulances were parked. Across the yard was

253

a tall wire fence with a collection of industrial buildings on the other side. Albigen quickly clambered up the fence and dropped down on the other side. Dante began to follow suit but he was not as good at climbing as Albigen.

'Hurry up!' Albigen called urgently from the other side.

Dante hesitated as the fence swayed precariously under his weight. The security guards were on the other side of the yard now. He scrambled up to the top, put one leg over, then the other and began climbing down.

'Just drop!' Albigen yelled.

Halfway down the fence Dante lost his footing and fell, turning his ankle. Albigen hauled him to his feet but Dante yelped as a lance of pain shot through his leg.

'What's the matter?'

'My ankle. I can't put any weight on it.'

'Lean on me,' Albigen said, desperately.

'It's no good,' Dante said. 'I can't run. Forget about me!'

'I can't!'

'You have to!'

The two security guards had reached the top of the fence and were turning to climb down.

'Go!' Dante urged.

Albigen hesitated. Then he made up his mind. 'Good luck, Dante!' he said. Then he fled while Dante stood and waited as the security guards surged towards him.

THE STAR CHAMBER

Guards dragged Dante back to the hospital and threw him into a tiny windowless room not much larger than a cupboard. He sat on the floor, hoping that Albigen had succeeded in getting away and would be able to make his way back to the Púca without the van. His ankle still hurt, and already the skin around it had turned purple, but it was not broken, only sprained. He was furious with himself and worried obsessively about Bea. Would she recover? If she did, would they punish her? Might she spend the rest of her days locked in a cell? Or would they merely content themselves with giving her Ichor and returning her to her parents?

At last, the door opened and a soldier stood in the entrance, holding a rifle and eyeing Dante grimly, as though confronting a dangerous animal. 'Outside!' he ordered.

A group of his colleagues waited in the yard. Beside them stood an army truck, its engine already running. Without another word, Dante was bundled into the back and driven off at top speed.

It was impossible to tell where they were heading since there were no windows in the back of the truck, but the journey seemed to last for hours. After a while

Dante fell asleep, waking later with a raging thirst to find the truck still hurtling along.

At last they came to a halt and the door was flung open. Dante climbed gingerly out and found himself in the courtyard of an enormous stone building. Dozens of narrow windows looked down on him like so many lidless eyes. But there was no time to take in his surroundings. He was quickly led through the entrance and along a series of panelled corridors to a huge pair of double doors guarded by yet more soldiers. There was a brief pause while the officer in charge presented his papers to the guards. Then the doors were opened and Dante was pushed inside.

The room in which he now found himself had been built in the shape of a six-pointed star with the entrance at its head and windows at the apex of each of the remaining points. It was unfurnished except for heavy velvet curtains at the windows and an elaborate chandelier hanging from the ceiling. The floor was of bare wood, and in the very centre of the room a circle had been marked with red paint. The officer led the way to the middle of the room until he and Dante were standing within this circle. The remaining soldiers took up positions at each point of the star, crouching down on one knee, their guns pointed in Dante's direction.

'Listen carefully,' the officer told him. 'You will remain within this circle at all times. My men have instructions to shoot if you take even one step outside. Is that perfectly clear?'

Dante nodded.

'Good.' The officer stepped backwards out of the circle, keeping his eye trained on Dante. A few moments later, a man in a wheelchair came into the room. His hair was grey, his skin was as white as paper and he seemed barely more than a skeleton. Yet there was something incredibly familiar about him. Suddenly Dante gasped. Ezekiel had been wrong! Sigmundus was not dead!

'So this is Yashar Cazabon's son,' the old man said. His mouth scarcely moved, yet his voice was oddly powerful.

Dante stared back with as much defiance as he could muster. 'Yes I am,' he said, 'though you tried your best to keep me from learning the truth about her.'

'It would have been far better for you if that knowledge had remained buried,' the old man continued. 'Instead, you have presented me with a problem. But every problem is also an opportunity, though I doubt very much whether you will enjoy the proposed solution.'

'What are you going to do with me?' Dante demanded.

There was a long pause. 'Tell me, Dante Cazabon, how do you think your mother died?' the old man asked.

'I know how she died,' Dante replied. 'She was murdered by you, or by people acting on your orders.'

'Ah! One of our friend Ezekiel's little fantasies, I'm afraid. The truth is that your mother threw herself from the top of the tower on Tarnagar by her own choice'

'That's a lie!' Dante shouted. 'You killed her.'

'You know, you really shouldn't believe the words of a madman.'

'He's not mad!'

The old man raised one eyebrow. 'Perhaps not, but Ezekiel Semiramis does not know quite as much as he thinks he does. Let me tell you about your mother. She was a very talented woman. All by herself she developed the ability to step outside the tiny little world to which you poor humans are confined. She learned to impose her will upon the energy that underlies all things.'

'Until you killed her!'

'I had no intention of killing her. As a matter of fact, I wanted to keep her alive for ever. That was what I offered her. The decision to die was hers and hers alone.'

'What do you mean you wanted to keep her alive for ever?'

'Just what I say. But she was so determined to resist me. Such a waste!' His voice sounded full of regret. 'She had so much potential. You see, only a tiny number of human beings possesses the ability to venture beyond their limitations. And it is that ability that allows me to make use of them.'

Dante stared at him in confusion. What had the old man just said? Slowly a terrible idea began to dawn upon him. 'Who are you, really?' he asked.

'I ask the questions,' the old man replied.

'You're not Sigmundus at all, are you?' Dante demanded. 'Ezekiel was right. Sigmundus is dead.

You're just using his body.'

A low noise emanated from the thing in the wheelchair. It took him a moment to realise that the creature was laughing. 'How very observant of you, dear boy,' it continued, 'and how very like your mother.'

Dante turned to the soldiers who surrounded him. 'This isn't your leader,' he cried. 'This is just a puppet.'

They completely ignored him.

Again there came that sinister, inhuman laugh. 'I'm afraid that none of them can hear you. You see, you and I are outside their little world for the time being. For everyone else here, time stopped at the moment this worn-out and withered body was wheeled into the room.'

If the creature that faced him was not Sigmundus, then what was it? Suddenly Dante remembered Perdita's warning. He thought of Eugenius's expressionless face and he was seized by an overwhelming panic. He would have run from the room, but found that he was pinned to the spot.

'As I was saying,' the creature continued, 'your mother was a remarkable woman. After she was gone, I believed there would never be another with so much ability. Until recently that is, when I felt the most extraordinary disturbance in the Odyllic world.'

'From Ezekiel?' Dante suggested.

'I'm not talking about your so-called friend,' the creature replied scornfully. 'I am only too familiar with the pathetic disturbance he creates. Every time he enters the world of the Odyll he leaves his filthy footprints. No, I'm talking about someone who is not yet fully aware of his own ability.'

'You mean me?' Dante demanded.

'I certainly do.'

Dante shook his head. 'You're making a mistake,' he said, quickly. 'There's nothing special about me. I'm a failure, a nobody.'

'You are quite unaware of your own potential, the creature continued. 'And that is precisely what makes you such an attractive proposition. It's rather charming, actually, a kind of innocence.'

'I don't have any potential,' Dante insisted.

'Oh, but you do. That was perfectly clear the moment you entered the world of the Odyll. I saw immediately why Ezekiel Semiramis risked everything to bring you out of Tarnagar. He thought he was rescuing you but the truth is, he was doing me a favour. Ironic, don't you think?'

'Look, it's true that I came awake in my dreams once,' Dante replied. 'But I don't know how I did it and I couldn't repeat it. If I could find my way back to the Odyll, don't you think I would've used it to escape?'

'You can find your way back, Dante. All you have to do is open your mind and let me guide you.'

'Never!'

'I'm afraid you don't have any choice.'

Suddenly Dante could see the lines of force radiating outwards from the body slumped in the wheelchair. The floor, the walls, even the windows blazed with them. A seething mass of energy, they surged across the room, writhing over the motionless bodies of the soldiers. Never had these living patterns of energy appeared with such furious intensity, and at last he understood what Ezekiel had tried to tell him: the world itself was no more than the shape that the patterns assumed.

Now the energy was everywhere, sparkling and crackling in the air he breathed. Every cell in his body was humming with its power as it leaped from one point to another like fire. He realised with a terrible certainty that there was no barrier left between himself and any other consciousness in the room. The doors of his mind stood open.

The creature spoke again. 'You are quite correct: there is absolutely nothing you can do to resist me.' It laughed, a mirthless peal of triumph.

Just as it could look into Dante's mind, so he could see directly into its thoughts and he knew that it was a thing of pure malice, concerned exclusively with its own survival. Sigmundus was no more to it than a point of entry into human society, a wound in the world that it had fastened upon. But the body it inhabited would not last much longer and the creature was ready to move on, like a virus that has chosen its next host.

He could feel how much it craved this process of absorbing another being's mind and he realised that it would not simply take him in one annihilating act. Instead it would feed upon him slowly for years, consuming him from the inside, feasting upon his anguish and pain.

Weakness began stealing over Dante like a tide coming into a beach. It became a struggle to remember who he was or what he was doing there. He forced himself to think clearly. 'My name is Dante. My mother was Yashar Cazabon,' he told himself.

As he thought this, there came sense of recoil and a loosening of the oppression that enveloped him. Like a man suffocating in a burning building who suddenly comes across a pocket of air, Dante's mind cleared for a moment. In that instant he recalled what the creature had said: that he possessed great potential, that he had caused a huge disturbance in the Odyll. Could he summon this power to fight back in some way?

Aware of what was going through his mind, the creature began to react. It was as if an alarm bell had begun ringing in the room, so insistent and clamorous was the anxiety that rose immediately to the surface of its mind. 'Any attempt to resist will only make things far worse for you,' it warned him.

But Dante detected something false about its tone, as if it was seeking to conceal some important information. 'What's the matter?' He flung the thought back at the creature. 'Have I got you worried?'

The creature's answer came in a roar of anger and a redoubling of its efforts to impose itself upon him. In return, Dante struggled to put aside his fear and focus his mind on reaching out towards those patterns of energy, taking control of them, forcing them to bend to the shape of his will.

He felt something hit him like a hammer blow, so hard that he reeled from the impact. It was the creature's anger, directed at him like a lightning bolt of pure rage and he felt it rearing up in front of him now, like a wall of water threatening to drown him. In a moment he would go under, swallowed up in those inky depths.

The last flickerings of his resistance seemed about to be extinguished when a faint image came into his mind: a picture of a small grey door set in a wall, its surface covered in living hieroglyphics that formed themselves into swirling patterns moving faster and faster. He remembered how that door had appeared by itself in his waking dream and he recalled his conviction that beyond that door lay an extraordinary power.

With the last of his strength, he focused on the image, straining to summon it more firmly into existence. Gradually it began to take shape until there it was – directly in front of him! A doorway in the air! Flickering symbols dancing across its surface, whirling in concentric circles, drawing him insistently towards them. As he gazed deeper and deeper into the vortex, their meaning became clear. Behind that door lay all the power and strength he had never known he possessed; behind that door was his true self. He had only to reach out, touch it and it would all be his.

He willed himself to move and the force which had held his body in its iron grip began to weaken. The air was filled with a hideous scream as the creature strove to prevent him from touching the symbols.

At last Dante's fingers made contact with the door. There was an explosion of blinding white light, then silence. A woman's voice whispered in his ear, telling him that he could walk away and leave all this behind him. Nobody could stop him. And he knew she was right.

AUTHOR'S NOTE

Odyllic Force

The term Odyllic Force was first coined by Baron Karl von Reichenbach (1788–1869), at the beginning of the nineteenth century. Von Reichenbach, one of the most renowned scientists of his era, is best known for the discovery of a number of important chemicals including creosote, which is used for preserving timber, and kerosene, which is essential to rocket fuels. The money he made from these discoveries allowed him to pursue research into all sorts of other areas, including the phenomenon of sleepwalking. His findings in this field led him to suspect the existence of an unrecognised force that only affected certain sensitive human beings. He conducted complex experiments into the workings of this force and published detailed descriptions of his results. However, his conclusions did not meet with the approval of the scientific establishment and they were subsequently discounted and buried in obscurity.

Brian Keaney
London
July 2006

ACKNOWLEDGEMENTS

The author gratefully acknowledges the assistance of Arts Council England, the Royal Literary Fund and The Authors' Foundation in writing this book.